DANGER: HIGH EXPLOSIVES!

Danger: High Explosives!

Carolyn Hart

ISBN: 979-8-3372-0396-6

This edition published in 2026 by Open Road Integrated Media, Inc.
180 Maiden Lane
New York, NY 10038
www.openroadmedia.com

To Louise Beard Moore with great affection

DANGER:
HIGH EXPLOSIVES!

Prologue

Kathryn levered the crowbar behind the hasp of the lock and, when it jammed tight, pulled with all her weight. The bar quivered with tension. Grimly, her arms aching, she hung on, pulling, pulling.

Abruptly, the hasp tore loose from the doorframe. The counterbalancing tension gone, she stumbled backward to fall on the rocky ground. The crowbar clattered out of her hands and she heard it strike against the flashlight that she had set on the ground in front of the shack door.

She scrambled onto her knees and her gloved hands swept the ground frantically. Somewhere beyond the heavy cloud cover that obscured the stars, a waning crescent moon hung in the sky. But here no light glimmered from stars or moon.

Her hands found the crowbar and then the flashlight. She gathered them up and hurriedly pressed the flashlight switch. A brilliant beam of light flared. Quickly, she turned it off and then stood, blinder than before from the sudden sharp spurt of light.

Sweat beaded her face even though the night held a hint of winter chill. She stood and waited with a wild impatience for the after image of the light to fade from her eyes. When she could discern again the darker block of the shack from the darkness of the night, she reached out to push the door, ajar now from the removal of the hasp.

Her gloved hand was touching the planked door when she heard the scrape of a boot on gravel and then solid slow footsteps.

She half turned and saw the swinging blob of light about fifty yards away. The bright white beam danced among the huge earth-moving machines, throwing into stark relief the graders and bulldozers and cement mixers and trucks, illuminating about a half million dollars' worth of road-building equipment.

A night watchman!

It hadn't even occurred to her that there might be a night watchman.

The probing, darting light came nearer and nearer. An old voice called out suddenly, "Here, lady. Come back here, Mrs. Sue."

Then Kathryn saw the plump white-whiskered terrier trotting toward the shack. Toward her.

Kathryn pressed back against the splintery wood of the door. She felt the door move and she moved with it, slipping inside the shack. She turned and eased the door shut and leaned against it and listened to the slow footsteps come closer and closer.

She was trapped. If the watchman saw that broken hasp dangling from the staple, he would investigate.

A pulse fluttered in her throat. He was close now, so close. And then her breath seemed to stop as the old terrier snuffled and scratched against the wooden door of the shack.

Quickly, Kathryn pressed hard against the door, holding it against the curious snuffle of the dog. And she heard the old man stop, only yards away, and call sharply, "Come here, Mrs. Sue. There's nothing for you there,"

She pushed against the door with her right shoulder. Her left hand, holding tight to the crowbar, slowly rose. Her left arm bent and tensed.

"You come on now, Mrs. Sue." The old man's boots scuffed on the rocky ground. "You come now."

Kathryn listened, scarcely breathing. She was sure, almost sure, that the voice was moving away!

He whistled, then called gruffly, "The last time you cornered a rat, you got a nasty bite. You come now, Mrs. Sue."

The voice was moving away!

The old terrier gave a final *whuff* at the door, then slowly pattered after him.

Kathryn waited a long time in the dank, stuffy shack before she relaxed—and the crowbar eased through the air to hang limply from her hand. But she made no move even yet. She was too close to success to take any chances now.

She waited, feeling sure now that she would succeed, that it was meant to go her way. She stood in the utter blackness of the shack and she remembered the flicker of the television film. It was the local news coming on and she had risen to walk across the room and turn off the set—and a feature had begun on the university ROTC's drill! She had stopped and stared at the set as if she could will the film to stop. The camera focused on the armory, squat and massive. Her throat tightened until she could scarcely breathe. It was an abomination, an evil. It should be destroyed. It was a cancer on the university.

When the film was over, still she stood, staring at the screen. The bland-voiced newscaster, suave and unctuous, smiled at his unseen audience. "Now we have a special report from our county correspondent, Ted Douglas, on progress of the new Interstate taking form east of town."

Another film began and huge road-building machines pushed and shoved earth and trees. A maelstrom of dust puffed and swirled from the onslaught of the graders and bulldozers. The newsman's voice rolled along with the film: ". . . believe this section of the new highway will be completed on schedule before Christmas although construction has been somewhat slowed by the unexpectedly wide ridge of granite encountered near Morristown. However, Paulson and Sons estimates . . ."

Kathryn had walked to the set and was leaning down to switch it off when a hill exploded on the screen. Her hand fell away from the knob. She watched the rest of the film carefully, intently.

And she felt again, as she stood in the darkness of the shack, that it was meant to be. The film of the armory. The film of a hill disintegrating.

She waited until long after she heard the watchman's footsteps cease in the distance. When there was no sound at all from outside, she turned on her flashlight and swiftly moved it all around the shack. No windows. She stood at ease now, safe from detection, and slowly beamed the light back and forth until she found what she sought.

The shiny yellow 50-pound wooden boxes were stacked neatly along the back wall. The sign above them warned:

HANDLE WITH CARE

DANGER

HIGH EXPLOSIVES

1

IT COULD DO NO HARM

Barbara Murphy clutched the twine-wrapped parcel tightly in her left hand. She balanced her notebook, an American history text, a collection of Lamb's essays, a sack of orange creams, and her roommate's mail under her right arm. She made it to the third floor of the dormitory, but when she opened the door, awkwardly twisting her right hand to turn the knob, the inevitable avalanche occurred.

Suzie Torres looked up from her book with a smile, unsurprised by her roommate's clattery arrival. She watched what looked like hundreds of leaflets slip and slide across the asphalt-tile floor along with the orange creams and books and letters. Her smile widened and she pushed up out of her chair to come help gather up.

She stood and looked down at Barbara, who was patiently picking up leaflets, one by one, and said mildly, "I scarcely know where to begin. What is it? A scrap-paper drive?"

Barbara paused and said reproachfully, "Suzie, these are the leaflets! They tell about the march." Barbara sat back on her heels, her hands full of leaflets, her earnest good-natured face glowing with excitement. "Haven't you heard about the march, Suzie? It's really going to be something! Everybody's supposed to come tomorrow afternoon, kind of like a picnic. I mean, it's a march and fun, too! You know, marching and songs and Frisbees and bubble gum all together on the Greenway."

Suzie knelt and began to stack the slippery sheets. Her voice held only a gentle hint of laughter when she observed, "That will take quite agile marchers, won't it, dear?"

Barbara's round face puckered and she said plaintively, "You know what I mean, Suzie. We're going to show the university we want love instead of war." Her nearsighted eyes blinked, then flickered toward the picture that sat on her desk. "Won't you help me pass out the leaflets, Suzie?"

Suzie's throat ached suddenly and she felt a sharp surge of anger at herself. The picture was of Barbara's brother, round-faced and earnest. He had stepped on a land mine eleven days before he was due to be rotated home from Vietnam.

"Of course, I'll help," Suzie said quickly and she patted and stacked the blue sheets into a neat pile. When all the sheets were gathered up, the slim black-haired girl scanned one. The simple message was proclaimed in block letters: ROTC NO! PEOPLES' PICNIC, 2 P.M. WEDNESDAY ON THE GREENWAY. LOVE, NOT WAR!

She arched a sleek black eyebrow sardonically, then shrugged. Oh well, it could do no harm. And it would make people like Barbara feel useful and involved.

Martin took a last hungry drag on the stub of his cigarette, then ground it out, ignoring the flicker of pain as his thumb and forefinger mashed the still-burning shreds.

"We need at least five hundred kids on the Greenway by two

o'clock." And he looked around the shabby living room at Kathryn and Ralph and Tim and Bob. "You can do it. Fan out, hit all the housing units. Keep your pitch light. Give it the old love come-on. Tell them this is the way to show they want peace. Tell them there will be beer and bubble gum and flowers—and make sure you pass out those brochures with the pictures of the Vietnamese kids who've been burned by napalm. Tell them it's little enough to do, to come to the Greenway to show they don't want little kids fried."

Kathryn leaned forward and her soft silky black hair curled around her face. She framed a question in her mind, then hesitated and her chance was lost because Martin was speaking again. ". . . try to make it look like any trouble is started by the cadets." He looked carefully at each of them. "Now that's essential or . . ."

Kathryn sat back, disappointed. This wasn't the time to tell him. But one of these days they would all be very proud of her, and her mouth curved in an eager smile.

Martin was too full of his own plans this afternoon to pay much attention to Kathryn. He straddled a straight chair and in a way looked so casual and easy with his cotton-blond hair and wheat jeans. But he moved through his days as tense and lithe as a marauding panther, and the smooth un-lined skin of his face masked a monumental arrogance that dismissed as totally unimportant the hopes and needs of others.

Billy Kessler laughed and the full-bodied roar of his mirth boomed in the small basement room.

His blond wife lifted her narrow pointed face from her needlepoint. She was so delicately built that her flesh seemed a luminous sheath over her small bones. She looked at her big Billy, at his thick chestnut-brown hair that tufted around his ears and at his full-blown luxuriant beard that seemed to have an ebullient life of its own. She looked at him and was shaken by a fierce flood of tenderness, but her voice was light and uninflected when she asked mildly, "What's so funny, Billy?"

He took a big booted foot and shoved it against his desk to whirl his swivel chair around until he faced her. Then he held up two sheets of paper and an envelope. "These'll teach me not to take myself too seriously as the editor of an underground newspaper." And he tossed the papers to her.

Annette glanced at the blue-and-gray insignia, the university's crest, in the upper-left-hand corner of the envelope, then she quickly scanned the two sheets. It was a handout from the University News Service, justifying the continuance of ROTC on the campus as a public service.

Billy was leaning back in his swivel chair, his bearded face tilted up to look at the ceiling, his generous mouth still stretched in a smile. She pushed out of her rocker and walked to the desk and glared down at him. She was angry—and she was never angry with Billy. "I don't see one single thing funny about calling ROTC a public service!"

He grinned and pulled her down in his lap. "You missed the joke, honey! Don't you see the irony?" He took the story back from her. "This is a news release from the University News Service!" Then he took the envelope from her hand and pointed to his name. "Look at that! Addressed to William Kessler, Editor, The Wilderness Voice, 419½ Oxford Street." He shook his big head. "Here I am, tilting at the Establishment, gallantly going forth to do battle daily with all humbug and self-serving double-talk, editing an unlicensed and unofficial newspaper—and I'm on the mailing list of the University News Service!"

He rumbled with laughter again and this time Annette smiled, too.

* * *

On the second floor of Pulitzer Hall, Jake Stuart, the fall-term editor of the university's campus newspaper, the *Gazette*, stared at the wall behind his desk. But his eyes were unfocused and the bright colors of the posters were only vague splotches at the edge of his consciousness.

Should he endorse tomorrow's protest rally? Should he warn against violence? Should he urge everyone to come who wanted peace? Or should he tell them all to stay home, that the organizers of the rally were suspect?

But he knew they would come. A lot of kids had had enough. More than enough. The Tet Offensive. My Lai. Cambodia. Kent State. The Pentagon Papers. The Winter Soldiers.

So much. Too much. And right here on the campus, they had a symbol of it all. The Reserve Officers' Training Corps. So they would come. But the spirit in which they came could make a world of difference.

Jake poised his hands over his typewriter. He began to type, slowly at first, then faster and faster.

When he had finished, he read the two sheets of copy carefully, thought for a moment, then added a final paragraph: *So if you gather at the Greenway to oppose ROTC or to support ROTC, bring your tolerance along with your beer.*

2

RALLY ON THE GREENWAY

They strolled along, carrying blankets and folding chairs and thermoses, guitars and brown bags and six packs, Frisbees and beach balls and bullhorns. It was a holiday crowd, good-natured and laughing.

". . . no kiddin'! What I mean is, if you're gonna do this ROTC stuff and be a damn officer, then, man, you better learn more than the manual. You know how many officers been shot in the back by their own EMs? Man, the *Wilderness Voice* lays it . . ."

Jake Stuart heard the rise and fall of the soft drawly voice as he hurried along the edge of the sidewalk. Jake shot a swift sideways look and saw an immense young man with shoulder-length hair and an Indian headband. His companion, wearing a velvet cloak, was nodding in vigorous agreement.

Jake grinned, then moved on past and drew even with a boisterous group that was laughing so hard they had stopped in the middle of the sidewalk and were trying to hold each other up.

"That's the ticket, Brownie," one of them gasped. He shoved his hair back out of his eyes. "That's what we'll do! If we can make Fitch break up laughing, he'll end up with so many demerits he'll drop ROTC. Look, here's how well . . ."

The group drew into a huddle that split apart in only an instant with howls of laughter.

Jake moved past them, but a smile lingered on his face and he didn't walk quite so fast. Everything was going to be all right. These were good kids. They were coming to the Greenway because they opposed armies and war and the training of men to kill, not because they wanted a hassle.

Nobody was going to get hurt.

And they came by the hundreds, filling the sidewalks, spilling over into the streets. They came laughing.

The Greenway stretched for two hundred yards north of the armory. Magnificent sycamores and smaller maples and thick-trunked elms lined the sides of the gently sloping field and topped the ridge to the west.

The kids spread across the northern end of the Greenway. Most of them never even noticed the two University Patrol cars parked across Frost Boulevard in the lot west of the Architecture Building.

It was an Indian summer day, the air deceptively mild, its true October chill bared only in the occasional gusts of wind.

Blankets and ponchos made bright splashes of color on the thick winter-pale grass. Red and yellow Frisbees skimmed through the air. A touch-football game ranged up and down in the middle of the field.

A girl with hair the color of an August moon softly strummed a guitar and sang a peace song in a haunting voice.

Those near her fell quiet. Slowly, one by one, other voices joined hers. Soft voices. Young voices. And over the well-kept Greenway the sound rose as clear as church bells on a windless Sunday morning.

Frisbees fell and were not picked up. The football bounced and rolled to a stop. The young clear voices rose and it was a cry of anguish and heartbreak.

". . . no more fighting, no more war . . ."

Then over the song, louder, stronger every second, came the cadenced slap of shoes on concrete.

"Hut, two, three, four. Hut, two, three, four."

The cadets came marching down Hurlburt Street, marching from their rally point behind the Student Union toward the Greenway, their drill field every Wednesday afternoon.

"GI beans and GI gravy. Gee, I wish I'd joined the Navy. Sound off, one, two. Sound off, three, four. Cadence count, one, two, three, four. One, two. Three, four!"

The singing on the Greenway stopped. Almost as a body, boys and girls pushed off from the grass and stood, waiting for the cadets.

"Hut, two, three, four. Hut, two, three, four. Hut."

On they came, march, march, march, as young in their uniforms as those who waited.

Jake Stuart felt the mood on the Greenway change. A great quiet settled over the waiting kids. The quiet reached out and touched the cadets as they marched down the street, ever closer to the occupied Greenway.

The battalion commander called out, "Sound off." Then, as he drew near enough to see those closed faces, he opened his mouth to chant but no words came.

The cadets marched on. As the beat came around again, the commander called, "Sound off," and then he improvised, "I wondered where the hippies went. They went to see the President. They all marched through the great White House and dammed if they could scare a mouse. Sound off."

The silence held but it was a tight and angry silence now.

Martin Henley jumped up on a park bench and swung a megaphone up to his mouth.

"Cannon fodder," he shouted.

"Cannon fodder, cannon fodder, cannon fodder . . ." The kids yelled and chanted and clapped their hands.

The cadets had reached the north end of the Greenway now. They stood, about fifteen companies each with forty men, and marched in place.

Jake felt a quick spark of admiration for the battalion commander, a skinny black-haired guy named Arthur Maguire. Sweat beaded Maguire's face and triangular patches of sweat stained his brown khaki shirt, but he didn't falter.

"Cadets, forward march," Maguire called and the column moved smartly south on Hurlburt.

Martin Henley jumped down from the bench and ran to the sidewalk that paralleled Hurlburt. "Move, everybody, move. Keep pace. This land belongs to the students, not to the war machine. Let's keep 'em off the Greenway."

Henley was running alongside the column, motioning for everybody to follow. And the kids began to understand and some of them were running now.

Jake broke into a run, too. He could see what Maguire hoped to do. He was going to lead the cadets to the south end of the Greenway and try to get on the field there.

But Henley saw it, too. He ran and called and worked his way along the sidewalk like a determined sheep dog.

So, by the time Maguire called, "Company halt. Right face," at the south end of the Greenway, he was again blocked by hundreds of kids.

Jake Stuart was trying to push through the crowd. He couldn't see what was happening up front. What was Maguire going to do now? If he tried to march onto the Greenway, he'd have to do it over the demonstrators. But if he didn't . . .

"Damn the colonel!" Major Skelly said viciously. Colonel Loomis had deliberately planned a golf game when he'd picked up word about the protest rally. The colonel wasn't about to face trouble. He wanted everything quiet and easy. This was his retirement post, an inglorious end to an undistinguished career, and he wanted only to get it over with. If there was to be trouble, let Major Skelly handle it. But the major hadn't given up on his own career. If he could wangle Leavenworth for his next assignment, there might even be a star someday. But there sure as hell wouldn't be anything but a loused-up efficiency report if he couldn't handle an ROTC drill!

He usually stayed near the end of the column. He liked to let the battalion commander handle drill while he wandered about, easy and cool, with just the right amount of skeptical humor and patience. But now he was running on the east side of the column, trying to see what was happening at the far end of the street. He stopped finally and climbed up on a park bench across the street from the Greenway. He could see Maguire and the hard-packed mass of demonstrators.

Damn them, the major thought. He turned and looked back toward the Architecture Building and the two university patrol cars. Skelly felt like shaking his fist at them. He hoped the campus cops were enjoying the show. He looked all around, but there was no help anywhere. And he didn't see any way on God's little green earth that Mother Maguire's boy Art was going to be able to handle this mess. Or Mother Skelly's boy, either!

But the loud-mouthed slobs weren't going to get away with it. Not if he could help it. He jumped down from the bench and ran alongside the column toward the end of the street. He passed the head of the column and turned right and ran along the sidewalk in front of the armory. Just ahead were three wooden barracks, WWII relics. His goal was the center one used by Army ROTC for offices and classrooms.

He slammed through the wooden front door, ignored the startled look from Miss Ogilvie, the clerical staff, and bounded down the hall to his own office. Yanking up the telephone receiver, he dialed 0 and waited impatiently for an answer.

"Operator, this is an emergency. Get me President Larsen on the line immediately. Army ROTC here."

He listened, then said angrily, "Well, if he's out of town, then get me somebody in charge. Quick."

While he waited, he stretched the telephone cord, but it wasn't long enough for him to be able to see out the window. The windows were closed but he could hear occasional yells and shouts.

"Dean Gorman speaking," announced a cigarette-scratched voice.

Prissy bastard, the major thought.

"Dean Gorman, this is Major Skelly. All hell's about to break loose over here on the Greenway. A mob of your woolly unwashed is blocking my cadets. I see two campus cop cars, but they aren't even trying to stop it. I don't much blame them. They're outnumbered. But I want somebody to come and get 'em out of our way."

Gorman didn't answer. His head throbbed. A sharp little pain jabbed behind his eyes.

"Dean?" the major said loudly. "What are you going to do?"

"I'll be right over."

"I hope you hurry," Skelly replied. "And I hope you don't come by yourself."

The students were swaying back and forth, arm in arm. Jake Stuart kept trying to push his way into the tightly-packed mass, wanting to get to the heart of the story, wanting to be there when thin-faced Art Maguire made his move, but he couldn't squirm between the linked arms, the close-packed bodies.

The kids were singing again, but it sounded like a different song. Their voices were loud, demanding. ". . . no more fighting, no more war . . ."

Jake gave up trying to shove his way forward. Instead he turned and began to run toward the slope that inclined gradually at first, then steepened abruptly into a bluff. And he rushed headlong into big Billy Kessler.

Billy grabbed his shoulder with a massive hand. "Hey, Jake, the action's back the other way."

Jake shook his head. "You can't get through, Billy. I'm going up on the bluff so I can see what's happening." And he pushed past and scrambled up weathered rocks to the summit. When he turned to look down on the demonstrators and, beyond them, the massed cadets, he wasn't surprised to have Billy clamber up to stand beside him.

The demonstrators were chanting now. Loud and clear came the shout: "Hell no, we won't go, hell no, we won't go, hell no, we . . ."

Jake pulled a small pad out of his shirt pocket and began to scrawl notes in his own abbreviated fashion: approx. 250–300 demos / all kinds / hippies, beaded, bangled, barefoot / lib.

dems. / pretty girls / slick SDS / Henley / lots. indep. kids too / Maguire stuck / singing . . .

Billy's shadow darkened the page. Jake looked up to see his big, bearded friend slowly shake his head.

"That's conventional reporting, Jake. And it misses the whole story."

Jake stared at his friend. He and Billy had argued about this sort of thing before. They had been friends for a long time, first as freshmen together in a dorm in a bewildering new world, then for a while in the Journalism School. Jake had tried hard to persuade Billy to stay in the J School, but his big friend said it was all closed up, that it belonged to the Establishment. So Billy went his own way and almost everybody on the campus knew the big, bearded humanities major who edited the *Wilderness Voice*.

So Jake made a gentle reply. "And what do you think is the story, Billy?"

Billy gripped his arm. "Listen, Jake. They're telling you. Listen!"

Hundreds of voices yelled it now. "Hell no, we won't go, hell no, we won't go, hell no, we . . ." Louder and louder. It was a deep-throated angry defiant triumphant shout.

". . . hell no, we won't go . . ."

Billy's hand fell away. "They mean it, Jake. That's the story. Everybody's had it, from Cambodia to Kent to My Lai. The local color isn't even in it, the Frisbees and the bubble gum and love in the afternoon. It's hell no, we won't go. That's your lead. That's your story."

Jake stared somberly down at the surging demonstrators. "That's a lot of the story, but not all of it. Look down there near the front, Billy." And he pointed where the crowd was thickest. "There's Henley with the megaphone and, man, look at him lead the cheers. And look at that redheaded guy that runs with

Henley, look at his face. That's hate, Billy. And over there, close to the armory, see that fat little guy in the yellow turtleneck? He hasn't missed a march for three years."

Billy frowned. "I see three hundred kids down there, Jake." He slowly shook his head. "You aren't listening."

Jake stared down at the swaying mass of demonstrators. Their chant shook the air. It thundered in his mind.

Art Maguire had had enough. He turned and shouted, "Right face. Forward march," then moved swiftly to the head of the column. Maguire's determined cadence call sounded loud and clear above the angry roars of the demonstrators.

"'It's Tommy this, an' Tommy that," and "Chuck 'im out, the brute"! But it's "Saviour of 'is country," when the guns begin to shoot.'"

Jake flashed a grin at Billy as they scrambled down the bluff. "Art's doing himself proud. You wouldn't think a business major would have enough cool to quote Kipling."

"O ye of little charity," Billy chided. "For a trade-school man, you're mighty condescending to the business college."

"*Touché.*"

Then the two friends began to run in earnest toward the north end of the field. They reached it at the same time as the head of the column of cadets—and most of the demonstrators. And, again, Art Maguire was stymied by a close-packed mob that wasn't going to let him pass.

He and the cadets stood stiffly in the bright October sunlight—and most of them were angry.

It was going to break apart, Jake realized suddenly. Some kid was going to rush the cadets or one of the cadets was going to break rank and then it would be up for grabs.

Abruptly a siren squalled high and higher, demanding

attention. And everybody looked north and here came the two University Patrol cars. For a moment, for a terribly important moment, everyone's attention was captured.

The first car, a brown-and-white Chevrolet with stenciled side panels—UNIVERSITY POLICE—rolled slowly past the cadets and nosed itself in between the column and the crowd at the edge of the Greenway.

Eben Petrowski, the lanky crewcut chief of the campus police, opened the driver's door and unfolded his long length out of the seat. He slammed the door, went around to the front of the car and climbed up on the right fender.

"Now hear this. Now hear this."

Petrowski had been a chief petty officer on a submarine until his retirement from the Navy three years ago. But he didn't cut a military figure. He wore brown slacks and a yellow-and-brown checked sports shirt. He didn't need a uniform and epaulets to lend authority. He stood on that fender like it was a ship deck and his voice was clear, flat, calm—and commanding.

"We seem to have a traffic jam here this afternoon, but it will all sort out easily enough. Demonstrators will gather, repeat, will gather on the north end of the Greenway and proceed with their demonstration. Cadets will march, repeat, will march into the center sector of the Greenway and proceed with their drill. Move quietly now and assume your stations."

For a moment no one responded. Then Art Maguire shouted, "Column half left, march!" and the cadets began a march that would take them diagonally across the Greenway to its center.

Chief Petrowski was urging the demonstrators, "This way, if you please, ladies and gentlemen. Let's share the land. Let everybody do his thing. Back this way, please, ladies and gentlemen."

And the kids started to move back, making way for the marching cadets.

A wide expanse of grass began to show between the demonstrators and the cadets.

But Martin Henley wasn't done yet.

"It's a trick," Henley yelled. "Don't let the cops push you around. Come on, this way! It's our land. Don't let the war machine on our land."

Henley was yelling and gesturing and some of the kids began to follow him, moving out into the belt of grass toward the marching column.

"Ladies and gentlemen." The flat, clear voice, unemotional but determined, sounded above Henley's calls.

Again, most of the kids stopped to listen.

Petrowski stood, arms akimbo, and said to Henley, "We seem to have a misunderstanding. This northern section is reserved for demonstrators. The central sector is now in use by the ROTC."

"No ROTC anytime, anywhere," Henley yelled. "And the only way you're going to stop us is to shoot us."

"You are quite free to demonstrate," Petrowski responded sharply, "and I won't let anybody stop you. Just like I won't let anybody stop the cadets from drilling."

"There's not enough room on this campus for ROTC," Henley shouted. "And you can't con us from blocking the drill. We're through being channeled and levered and controlled. We're going to shove those cadets right off the Greenway."

He turned his back on Petrowski. The wind whipped his white-blond hair. He thrust his strong-boned face forward and yelled, "Don't let murderers bluff you with good manners! They use napalm on little kids in Vietnam because they don't give a damn. Well, we do. We care and we're going to kick the war machine right off the campus. So, come on! Don't let them suck you in. They're killers. All of them. Come on!" It was a scream for attack, and he turned and began to run toward the cadet column.

"Ladies and gentlemen!" Petrowski's voice boomed over the Greenway, drowning out even the measured cadence calls of the cadets and the yells of Henley's followers.

And, once again, the kids responded to the authority of Petrowski's voice and the just-begun surge toward the center of the Greenway slowed.

"Come on! Come on!" Henley shouted.

Kids milled back and forth, some responding to the chief's orders, others to Henley's impassioned calls. But no one could ever say with a clear heart what might have happened.

Nobody there ever forgot what did happen.

3

"THE HELL YOU SAY, GOERING!"

Dean Gorman was in the lead car. He wished to God they'd turn off the siren. But they didn't. He held onto the door handle as the patrol car slewed around corners.

Ah-waah-ah-waah-ah-waah.

He turned his head stiffly. It still throbbed from last night's martinis. He'd told Laura and told her not to ask people for dinner on a school night. And she laughed and said, "School night, dear? You aren't a child, you know. Though I sometimes wonder." And so he'd drunk a martini too many. Maybe even two too many. He squinted his eyes against the glinting brightness of the sun through the rear window and counted the string of cars. Five, six, no, by God, seven patrol cars and two paddy wagons!

That ought to take care of Major Skelly's emergency.

Then the throbbing in his head was surpassed by sharp angry pains in his stomach. He was going to look like the world's biggest fool if they screamed up to the Greenway and Petrowski had everything under control. Oh God, maybe he shouldn't have called the city police. Of all the afternoons for President Larsen to be out of town, why did he have to pick this one? But Skelly had called for help and he had to do something! Maybe he should have . . .

He hunched forward. There, at the north end of the Greenway, a ragtag disorderly mass of students was milling about and, beyond them, the cadets.

The cadets had stopped marching and had turned to face the protesters. As the police cars squealed up to the Greenway, cadets and demonstrators alike were yelling.

". . . ROTC get out!"

". . . our field, too, and we'll . . ."

"Murderers, murderers, mur . . ."

"Stupid potheads can . . ."

And over all of it sounded Henley's hoarse command, "Let's get 'em now. Now! Now!," and Chief Petrowski's calm plea, "That's right, ladies and gentlemen, very good now, back this way, if you please."

Dean Gorman clambered out of the car. His gaze swept over the long-haired, shabbily-dressed students, most of whom were turning back under the chief's urgings, and he felt a furious rush of anger that left him almost physically sick.

The dirty, ill-mannered, stupid louts. They didn't deserve to come to a university. He had worked in a fraternity-house kitchen and shoveled snow and carried groceries and, in the summers, he had sweated and strained in the oil fields, all for enough money to go to school so he could be somebody! His mother had put off going to the doctor until the pain was so bad so he could have every extra penny and make it through and get his degree. And when she had gone to the doctor, it was too late.

He stood at the edge of the Greenway on a warm and sunny

October afternoon twenty years later and the anger and the hatred washed through him.

He hated their clothes, made to look shabby. They didn't know what it was to be shabby, to jab your fingers with a needle trying to darn together cloth that had just worn itself out. They didn't know what it was to be hungry, actually not to eat breakfast or dinner because you didn't have enough money to buy food. They couldn't know how you grudged the nickel for a bar of soap but you bought it to be clean and neat, to be a university man.

They didn't know anything! He hated their grubbiness and long hair and the awful arrogant way they took the university to be their servant. They took it for granted that they could go to college!

The police jumped out of the long line of cars. Riot-helmeted, billy club-equipped, they began to form a line of attack.

Chief Petrowski was hurrying toward them. "Dean Gorman," he called, "we won't need the patrolmen. The kids are backing up. We won't . . ."

Gorman didn't even hear him. The police captain handed the dean a loudspeaker mike. Gorman took it.

"Get off the Greenway!" he screamed, his voice strident with fury. It reverberated across the Greenway, sounding like magnified thunder, like the voice of doom in a high-school play. It was so loud, so thunderous, it was almost unintelligible.

"Get off! Get off!"

Students who had begun to fall back at Chief Petrowski's urging turned and stopped and faced the source of that monstrous voice.

"Get off! Get off!"

Petrowski was pushing through the kids but he didn't reach the dean in time.

Gorman turned to the police captain. "Move in. If they don't break up right now, arrest them. Haul them all down to jail."

He looked up and saw the hand cameraman of Channel 9. The dean stood a little straighter and lifted his chin.

The cameraman was panning the whole scene now, the patrol cars parked all askew, the helmeted police moving slowly forward, the cadets watching, the formless mass of protesters, most of them retreating step by step.

Gorman spoke again, but his voice was lower now, smoother. The cameraman might have his own sound unit. This could be on the five o'clock news across the state tonight.

"The university will not tolerate violence," Gorman declared, each word carefully enunciated. "No students will be accorded special privileges. The field is to be cleared of everyone save cadets."

It didn't need SDS leaders to rouse the demonstrators now. A chubby, neatly-dressed graduate student shouted in his high precise voice, "The hell you say, Goering!"

And the kids took it up, delighted by this use of the name of Hitler's pal.

"The hell you say, Goering! The hell you say, Goering!"

The Greenway didn't belong to Dean Gorman. Who the hell was he to order them off? Goering?

And it was wonderful to watch Dean Gorman, to see the slow realization that the kids meant him and the conviction that from now on, forevermore, here or on another campus, the students would always call him Goering.

Suzie Torres watched his face and when the dean glanced wildly at the TV cameraman she knew that he was afraid a soundman might be picking up that taunting call to broadcast it across the state. God, across the nation!

Suzie grinned. It was worth coming just to have seen Dean

Gorman's face at that moment. But as the inexorable advance of the police continued, her smile faded and she pulled on Barbara's arm. The police were closer now, much closer. They were big well-built men in dark brown uniforms—and they held their billy clubs raised high.

Suzie pulled harder on Barbara's sleeve. But her friend, chanting loudly, "The hell you say, Goering!" tried to shake off her hand.

"Barbara!" Suzie cried sharply. "We'd better . . ." She broke off and frowned. What on earth was Billy Kessler doing? A long while ago, she had noticed him standing up on the bluff with Jake. When the action had moved back up the Greenway, she had lost track of both of them. And now here was Billy, making his way through the retreating kids, heading straight for the line of policemen.

Billy plunged through the crowd with both hands held high. For all the world, Suzie thought, as if he were getting ready to bless the fleet or baptize at the river. Dear Billy. Dear good Billy.

She looked from Billy back toward the advancing police and she saw the wariness in their faces, the tension in their upraised arms, and she screamed after her big friend, "Billy, stop! Billy, they'll hurt you, oh Billy, please stop!"

He heard her and looked back and shook his head. Then his deep voice boomed, "Wait, sir. Wait a minute! Let's all fall back."

Billy was only a few feet from the captain, Tom Bristow. Bristow was a big man, too. He stood six-foot-one barefoot but he had to look up to watch Billy. Bristow tightened his grip on his club and wished to hell he had a gun. The mayor was a damn fool with his order of no guns on the campus. A cop without a gun was like a big cat without claws, vulnerable. And how many cops had been killed so far this year across this wonderful land of the free and home of the bushwhacking cop killers? It was seventy-four at last count and this was only October.

Bristow arched his right arm higher and tensely watched the young giant striding up with a smile on his face. Some of them thought it was a laugh a minute to kill a pig.

He was watching Billy very closely so he didn't see the blurred movement high in the branches of the maple tree to his left. The October leaves, as rich with color as red wine prismed in a morning sun, still thickly cloaked the branches. The leaves shook as the bottle hurtled down. A few leaves fell.

The impact against Bristow's frontal bone felled the big man like a hammer blow. The men beside him saw him topple over, blood bright on his face. And they saw the hands of the big young man reaching out toward their falling captain.

The policemen plunged into the milling mass of demonstrators, their clubs swinging.

Suzie and Barbara saw Billy fall under the blows of the police. And they saw the line of patrolmen moving in, slamming down anyone in the way. Suzie grabbed Barbara by the arm and pulled her around. They tried to run but there were too many ahead of them. Most of the kids were trying to get away. Some, in a fury, tried to charge back against the police.

Barbara stumbled and lost her balance and began to fall. Frantically, Suzie yanked on her arm, raising her up on her knees. Pulling and dragging her friend, Suzie tried to push a way for them through the crowd. Behind her she could hear screams and thumps and, once, an awful splotting sound like a ripe melon rupturing.

The Channel 9 newsman was standing on the hood of the lead car and nobody was telling him to get off. He was trying to keep his camera steady, trying to get the whole thing on film. Fantastic pictures. They should really sack up a full-time job for him when he finished school in the spring. He zoomed in now, right into the center of the action, the kids running, the clubs swinging. Damn, what beautiful pictures!

University Police Chief Petrowski was yelling, "Wait! Stop! Wait!" but his voice couldn't be heard over the screams and shouts. Angrily, he began to run after the charging policemen.

Patrolman John Vossler swung his club methodically left and right, left and right. When it struck an arm or a back or elbow, the smooth hard swing jolted to a stop but only for a split instant. His hand gripping the haft would close even harder and, with a massive push, Vossler would force the club on, left then right, left then right.

He was breathing in short gasps, his mouth half open. He was terrified. Was it a sniper that got Captain Bristow? The captain, such a big strong man, had fallen so suddenly, blood blossoming on the front of his head like a bright crepe-paper flower.

Was there a sniper out there somewhere? Would the next bullet slam into his head, hurting unbearably for a tiny span, then would there be nothing? Nothing? Spit trickled down Vossler's chin but he didn't realize it. His shoulders ached from the tight bunching of muscles tensed to ward off the violent hurt of a bullet. Left then right, left then right, harder, harder. Left then right. He was nineteen years old.

Vossler's club was on its swing to the left, slicing upward with all the force of 180 pounds of muscle and bone powered by fear, when the rounded tip gouged its way across Barbara's right cheek and ear.

Her scream of pain pulled Suzie down beside her. The bubbling cry of anguish filled Suzie's mind so that she didn't see the bloodied club scythe by her, so very close, and then Vossler was past them, swinging left then right, left then right.

Barbara huddled on the autumn-browned grass, her blood-stained hands cupped over the side of her face. "Oh, it hurts so much. Please, please don't let it hurt so much. Ah, I can't stand it."

Tears slipped down Suzie's face as she held her moaning friend in her arms. Barbara had never hurt anybody, ever. Dear sweet silly dumb Barbara. Damn them. Damn the pigs.

And then, as suddenly as it had begun, it was over.

Petrowski, gray-faced, consumed by anger, had reached Dean Gorman and pulled the loudspeaker mike out of his hands and ordered in his flat controlled voice, "Halt. All units halt immediately."

The patrolmen heard that authoritative voice and obeyed. They stopped where they were and looked blankly about. Slowly they began to realize that no police, other than Captain Bristow, were injured but moaning students were scattered across the field. And some did not moan but lay still and quiet, crumpled as they had fallen.

4

"LOVE, MR. PRESIDENT?"

Jake typed savagely. He reached the end of a line and slammed the carriage back, then stopped and gripped the sides of the typewriter and waited for the fresh surge of anger to crest, then recede. He had never in his life been this angry. Who the hell did Gorman think he was? Ordering them, *ordering* them off the Greenway. As if they didn't matter. As if they were negligible! Well, the good dean was going to find out who was negligible—and who wasn't!

Jake glared at the paper in his typewriter, then abruptly yanked it out and crumpled it up and rolled in a fresh sheet.

He stared out through the glass partition that separated his office from the *Gazette* newsroom. He could see the startling red hair of Rusty Jacobs, the managing editor. Rusty was doing a half dozen things at once, talking on the phone, editing a story, nodding in answer to a reporter's question, keeping a check on the time and, most of all, riding herd on the multifaceted coverage of the biggest story to hit the *Gazette* in a decade.

And while he worked, his left hand pulled and pushed on that flaming frizzled mop of hair until it stood out from his head and looked like nothing quite so much as the bright orange fluff on a stuffed dragon's back.

The magnificent disarray of that great head of hair brought a faint smile to Jake's face—and it was the first time he had smiled in many hours. Then, impatiently, Jake looked back at his typewriter and started over.

He wrote angrily, bitterly, and well. He typed without pausing again and when he had finished he read his copy over, then slowly nodded. That ought to get that son-of-a-bitch Gorman. That ought to back him right up against the wall.

At that moment, Dean Gorman stood in President Larsen's office with his back literally against the mahogany-paneled north wall, driven there by the wildly waving arms of tiny Dean Abernathy, who was demanding pugnaciously, "Since the police were acting as your agents, Dean Gorman, how can you be deemed anything other than wholly responsible?"

Gorman blinked and his reddish face turned an even deeper color. "So it's all my fault! Well, I don't see it like that. How about the punks who wouldn't let the cadets on the Greenway? How about them? What kind of right do they have to keep the cadets off the Greenway? And how about the punk that threw the bottle? You act like I personally told those cops to knock everybody down. I just told them to clear the Greenway. If anybody got hurt, it wasn't my fault!"

Dean Abernathy threw his arms up in the air and his hands flapped angrily. "You brought the police on the campus! You sent them against our students! And you have the . . ."

"Gentlemen, gentlemen." His voice was dry and thin and mild but it had a special quality, the warmth of honest interest, and that warmth reached out and touched the two deans and Dean

Gorman felt less threatened and Dean Abernathy remembered suddenly that anger was uncivil and even, perhaps, unseemly.

"Now that we are all here," President Larsen said, "we can get our meeting underway," and he led, without seeming to, the two embattled deans back toward the center of the room and the long conference table. Five of the eight tall and beautiful chairs around it were already occupied by deans or vice-presidents.

President Larsen was taking his place at the head of the table when the double-doors at the far end of the room opened and Thomas Putney, the director of the University Office of Public Relations, stepped inside, looking quite worried and conspiratorial. He waved discreetly. "Mr. President, if I could speak to you for just a moment?"

Larsen looked down the room and thought that Tom Putney, had he been there, would have stopped Thoreau on his way to jail to report excitedly on the latest news from the Mexican War. But the irritation that flickered in his mind didn't reach his face and he decided quickly that it would be best to find out what was worrying Tom. His session with the deans and vice-presidents would run late into the night.

"Gentlemen, excuse me for a moment, please."

He walked briskly down the room, a small spare man just past sixty. Gray hair tufted around his balding head. He stopped at the door and inclined his head, then said in his clear voice, "Yes, Tom, I think you're right. I'll take the call at my desk."

When he lifted the receiver, his face was wary and intent, but he spoke pleasantly. "Mr. Stuart? As Mr. Putney explained to your reporter, there will be no official statement by the university until tomorrow. A press conference is scheduled at 9 A.M. in this office. Your representative . . ."

"Will be there, Mr. President," Jake interrupted, "but that won't help us tonight. The *Gazette* goes to press tonight. And we would hope to carry for our readers in the morning the response of our president to the uncalled-for violence against students on the Greenway."

President Larsen drew his breath in sharply. He paused, then said soberly, "I would think your statement a little misleading, Mr. Stuart."

"Would you?" Jake responded. "Were you on the Greenway this afternoon, President Larsen?"

"No. But I have been conferring with some who were there and . . ."

"Who?"

President Larsen paused, then said thoughtfully, "I have no wish to spar with you, Mr. Stuart. I well understand your desire for a statement. I would like to give you a statement. However, I learned many years ago not to draw conclusions from insufficient data. I returned to the campus only an hour ago from a trip out of town. Since I returned I have been very much involved in trying to determine what happened here this afternoon. As I said, I have spoken already to quite a few persons who were present. I have not yet, however, spoken to any of the injured students. I would wish to do so. At this moment, I am still gathering information."

"I've got the information," Jake replied. "I was there and I can tell you exactly what happened. Dean Gorman brought in the bully boys in brown and they attacked the kids—and beat hell out of them. That's what happened, Mr. President."

"That is not quite the whole story, Mr. Stuart."

"I'm sorry," Jake said tiredly. "I'm sorry for you and for the university and for the kids. For everybody. I'm just sorry as hell, Mr. President, but that is the story. And the *Gazette* has that story. Now it's up to you to decide whether part of that story will be the refusal of the university president to comment on what happened."

President Larsen stood very straight beside his desk. He stared for a long moment at the log fire crackling in the fireplace. He wondered at the edge of his mind who had started the fire. Probably that fool Tom Putney. It was a marvel that Putney wasn't handing out Scotch and soda and passing around peanuts. The logs shifted on the grate, a small one splitting apart, burned through. Once a fire catches, it quickly consumes logs. The older the logs, the faster they burn.

This bloody Wednesday could consume the university if it weren't controlled and dampened.

Kenneth Larsen was a tough man, but, more than that, he was a confident man. He spoke slowly, evenly.

"I would like for you to understand, Mr. Stuart, that I am not yielding to your pressure in order to make me look good or in order to protect Dean Gorman. I yield to your power because I hope, ultimately, to save the university."

He paused and thought for a moment, then said decisively, "This is my statement: I am actively seeking to discover the causes of the confrontation on the Greenway between police and students. I will talk to as many who were present as I possibly can. I will not do this in order to blame either students or administrators or law-enforcement officers. I will do this so that, with God's grace, we may understand what brought violence to our campus and thereby learn how to avoid violence in the future."

He frowned and looked down at the age-muted pattern of the rust-and-gold Persian rug, then continued gravely, "I seek the help of all the university, of the students, of the faculty, of the administrators, to work together to heal our campus."

The small spare man stood silently for a long moment, thinking, then he nodded. "That is my statement, Mr. Stuart," He hesitated, then made his appeal. "If you love your university, Mr. Stuart, you will work with me to keep this under control."

Jake didn't laugh. Not quite.

"Love, Mr. President? I think you have the wrong script. This isn't Mr. Chips and his old boys, you know. At last count, the university had 23,000 students and they all get bounced around like counters on a crap table. Somebody slips a card into the computer and ding-dong-bell a name comes out the other end. Love the university? That's like trying to make out with a robot. Maybe it could be programmed, like canned applause, but I'm afraid it'd be just about as much fun."

Larsen's silence this time was taut and angry. He rejoined crisply, "If you have no personal attachment to the university, Mr. Stuart, you might still be willing to consider its importance to the maintenance of civilization. If there is no tolerance or orderly exercise of opposing viewpoints on a university campus, Mr. Stuart, then pray tell me where opposing viewpoints will be able to meet?"

"The magic words," Jake said softly. "Opposing viewpoints. You make it sound so civilized, so important, President Larsen, and all you're really saying is that no matter how many people don't like it or how many students oppose it, you aren't anyhow or anyway going to kick ROTC off the campus. That's what you're saying, isn't it?"

"That's not quite all of what I am saying," the president replied quickly. "In fact, you have half of it. I won't kick ROTC off but I won't kick ROTC's opponents off, either. If you don't understand, Mr. Stuart, it's called tolerance."

Jake did laugh this time. A short hard laugh. "Tolerance," he repeated. "The kids got just about all the tolerance they could stand this afternoon."

The fluorescent tube that burned above President Larsen's head didn't diffuse much heat. Not enough, certainly, to account for the sweat that beaded the president's balding head.

He closed his eyes briefly and wiped the sweat off his forehead. Then he spoke, emphatically yet calmly, "If you wish to twist my meaning, you can easily do so. But I feel sure that you won't forget the training that has been yours, even as angry and unhappy as you are now. I trust that your editorial comment will be made in editorials and that your news columns will report what happened as accurately as possible. And now, Mr. Stuart, I must return to the conference table, but I will look forward to seeing you at the news conference in the morning."

"Yes, sir," Jake said slowly.

He held onto the receiver for a long moment after President Larsen had hung up. He stood there and felt very tired and uncertain. He had always prided himself on being absolutely accurate in his reporting. And he was accurate! He had told Larsen the way it really had been. Jake's shoulders straightened and the anger and the certainty flowed back into him. He jammed the receiver back into the cradle and swiped his sweaty hand on his pants leg—and immediately pulled his hand away as if it had touched spots of fire. Those dampish sticky spots splotched down his right pants leg—he had helped load Billy Kessler into an ambulance. Somebody had already wrapped a cotton shirt around one side of that battered head, but the blood had still run and dripped and splashed.

Jake held his right hand out away from him and stared at the sticky reddish-brown smear, and his last doubt as to the rightness of his course fell away.

5

"DAMMIT, IT'S TRUE!"

Time had ceased to have any meaning for Suzie. She felt as if she had been in the crowded hallways of St. Catherine's emergency ward forever, imprisoned by others' pain, soul-sickened by bloodied heads and bruised faces and broken bones.

St. Catherine's was doing its best. It wasn't yet up to serving as a field hospital after a battle engagement. The injured filled the six small examining rooms, two and three to each, and spilled out into the hallway, sitting and lying on the cold marble floor.

The kids waited with pain-filled eyes but in grim quiet. It was almost eerily quiet, with only an occasional rustle or low-voiced exchange. Each person seemed wrapped in his own thoughts, his own pain.

Suzie looked up and down the hall and wondered what each one thought. Was the girl in the long blue dress angry or full of hatred or frightened? And what about the boy next to her, the one with the velvet cape and the blood on his face?

Their faces gave no hint of their thoughts. And Suzie didn't know what they felt. She too sat quietly, turned inward, seeking to understand what had happened to her this afternoon. How was it that she had so little empathy with the others in that long hallway? She had been on the Greenway with them. She had turned and run from the clubs. But she had no sense of community with them.

She sat near the double-doors that opened out of the emergency ward into a main corridor of the hospital. She half-supported Barbara with her right arm. The boy directly across from her cradled his limp left arm in his right hand. He wore a blue denim shirt and black bellbottoms. His long brown hair curled softly around his ears. His sideburns flared, thick and furry at the ends. His face was gentle and civilized except for the hard set to his jaw.

He felt her gaze and looked toward her. He stared and his eyebrows knotted. She saw the puzzlement and the surprise and, strongly, the outrage in his eyes.

He looked at her and abruptly words shot forth. "They attacked us!" His voice was filled with incredulity. "I never believed it before."

At her puzzled look, he continued raggedly, "You know. Like the Panthers and the rock festivals and the blacks. They always said the police would beat you up, bust you even if you weren't doing anything. Well, I never believed it before." He stopped. His mouth quivered. "Well, dammit, it's true!" Tears brimmed in his eyes.

She looked at him, then gazed up and down the hall. Pain-filled faces had turned to listen and watch the boy. In every face, Suzie saw the same mingled look of outrage and disillusion and anger.

"Off the pig!"

The hoarse whisper came from the far end of the hall, but everyone heard it.

Automatically, without even thinking, Suzie shook her head.

"Off the pig!" came the implacable demand again. It was a primeval call, the ages-old lust for blood and vengeance.

"No," a voice said calmly, absolutely.

Suzie felt the strength and firmness of the command and even before she turned her head to look, she knew it was Billy.

"No," Billy Kessler said again, louder than before. And he pushed away from the wall and stepped into the center of the hall. "No. That isn't the way."

Annette, his thin blond shadow, held his left arm. She seemed to be trying to hold him up by his arm. He swayed as he stood there. A temporary bandage of a striped blue-and-yellow shirt swathed the right side of his leonine head. Blood had seeped through the cotton and was clotted thickly in his hair and beard. His right arm dangled. He didn't stand quite straight. He hunched forward as if his right shoulder was a burden.

"What's the matter?" the hoarse voice demanded. "You like to hurt? You got a martyr's complex? I say, give what you get. Off the pig!"

Billy teetered unsteadily but he managed to stay on his feet. It was so long before he answered that Suzie wondered if he had heard.

But answer he did.

"Killing is wrong," Billy said simply.

That was all he said, but the words hung in that wide hall with its dirt-streaked floor and human bundles of pain and anger. They hung there and expanded and each mind could hear the simple answer, "Killing is wrong."

Martin Henley heard Billy's answer as he stepped out of Examining Room 3, his right hand splinted. He was wild with impatience to be gone from the hospital but he paused and turned to watch and listen.

There was a rustle near where Martin stood, and a skinny kid pushed himself up from the floor. He too had only one hand he could use. His right arm dangled with that odd tilt that meant a broken bone, but he made it to his feet, then limped slowly up the hall until he stood face to face with Billy. He looked very small compared to Billy. He stood, frail and weedy, and looked up.

"They'd kill us!" he said accusingly. "They would've killed us if Petrowski hadn't stopped it,"

Billy nodded tiredly.

"Then for God's sake, what d'you want us to do? Stand there and let them kill us?"

It was a taunt, the most absurd possibility he could envision.

But again that big head nodded slowly. "Yes," Billy said. "If that's the way it must be."

The little guy blinked reddened eyes, then shook his head like a child with water in his ears who doubts his hearing. "You're crazy," he said finally. "Why the hell should we stand there and get killed?"

Billy's mouth quirked into a smile. "You told me why," he said gently.

"Huh?"

"For God's sake," Billy said simply. "Or however you want to put it. For the sake of life. For the sake of goodness."

His skinny little opponent smiled derisively. "Oh, yeah. You're some kind of religious nut, huh?"

Surprise flickered on Billy's face. "No. You don't hear me, man. I'm not talking about religion. I'm talking about living. I'm talking about what happens in your own life when you meet evil." He paused and groped for the right words. "Martin Luther King, Jr., he knew about living. And so did Gandhi. They both told us. They said that no matter how evil others might be, they would never be evil in return. They wouldn't hate. And they wouldn't hurt. Do you know why they told us that?"

The smaller boy said bitterly, "Because they wanted to be martyrs. Well, they got what they asked for."

"That's not right," Billy said sharply. "They liked to live, but they knew what really mattered in living, what mattered more than life."

The frail young man reached out and gripped Billy's left arm as the bigger youth swayed. The stridency was gone from his voice when he spoke. "That doesn't make any sense."

Billy blinked his uncovered eye and stared at the smaller boy.

"I'm not putting it very well," Billy began apologetically.

"Oh, you put it OK," the boy said hastily, kindly. "I get you. I just don't buy it. It's all this new stuff, this passive resistance stuff. But it just makes it easy for the pigs." And his voice hardened. "I say, don't make it so easy for the pigs."

Billy shook his head tiredly. "No. No. Don't you see? The ones who are trying to hurt you, they don't matter. What matters to you is what you do. The evil that you do will destroy you, not the evil that is done to you."

The skinny young man shook his head now in stubborn and total disagreement. "You're just off on a kick. They won't get you anywhere, all these slogans."

Billy smiled again. "They aren't slogans and the idea behind them isn't new. It's as old as man. Martin Luther King, Jr. didn't invent it or Gandhi or even Christ. It's a truth about living that man figured out a long time ago."

Billy took a deep breath and said, so softly that everyone strained to hear, "There was a Greek poet, Hesiod, who lived more than seven hundred years before Christ. Hesiod put it as well as anybody. He said, 'For himself doth a man work evil in working evils for another.'"

Then Billy moved away from his opponent, reaching toward the wall with his good left arm. "Conventional wisdom," he said softly, almost to himself. "But perhaps that's the best kind." And then he fell.

He was so big, so heavy, that he collapsed with a bone-jarring thud.

Suzie pulled her arm from around Barbara, who moaned and lifted her head.

"Just a minute, Barbara. I'll be right back. It's Billy. He's fainted."

As she scrambled to her feet, the incongruity of her words frightened her. How could Billy, big powerful Billy, faint? Oh God, how badly was he hurt? Why hadn't he been seen? Damn them all, if Billy suffered.

Annette crouched beside him, her thin hands cradling his battered head.

"Billy!" she cried, her voice shrill and desperate. "Billy. please!"

Suzie stood over Billy and Annette. The stone-gray pallor of Billy's face sent her stumbling frantically down the hall, stepping over and around the other injured.

"Sister!" she called. "Sister!"

The nun behind the desk moved so quickly her habit swirled. Sister Mary Margaret lived with crises. She knew the voice of crisis. By the time Suzie reached the desk, Sister Mary Margaret was already opening the door to Room 4.

"Dr. Baird," Sister Mary Margaret called. "Dr. Baird, quickly!"

Suzie heard a muttered response. It seemed a long time but it was only seconds before the doctor stepped out into the hall. He was young. His hair curled thickly on the nape of his neck. His face still carried a summer tan, but lines of tension splayed out from his eyes.

"This way!" Suzie cried. "He's fainted—and he's gray, a terrible color of gray!"

The doctor pushed past her and knelt by Billy and picked up a limp wrist. Then, frowning, he began very gently to disengage the makeshift bandage on Billy's head.

"My God," he said softly.

Suzie looked down, then turned away and pressed against the plaster wall. Numbly she heard the doctor, ". . . immediate surgery. Must've been in fantastic pain. See if . . ."

Then angrily, the young doctor demanded, "Why hadn't we seen him, Sister? He should have been one of the first to be treated." He looked down at his watch. "My God, it's almost seven o'clock! That kid's been here for hours with the side of his face like that!"

Suzie forced herself to turn back around. She saw the doctor, red-faced and angry, staring at the sister. She saw Billy, stretched out now on a wheeled table, his poor battered head gently braced. And she saw Annette, holding a big limp hand and saying in a tear-choked voice, "Please, Doctor, don't blame Sister. Billy kept saying there were others who needed help more. And he's so big and looks so strong that nobody thought he was badly hurt." She pressed that flaccid hand against her cheek and her words were muffled. "I didn't know it was so bad. We got separated when the police hit at everybody and I didn't find him again until I came to the hospital. I didn't know it was so bad."

Suzie stood and watched them and looked at that awful wound and tears slipped unheeded down her face. She turned and walked blindly back up the hallway. She couldn't help Billy now. Only a surgeon could help Billy.

She came to the place where she had left Barbara and stopped and looked about.

"They took your friend a few minutes ago," the boy in the

blue denim shirt volunteered. "They said they were going to sew up her ear, then keep her overnight for observation."

Suzie nodded. "Thank you," she managed. She reached down and picked up her shoulder bag, then stood uncertainly. She had been there for so long, she couldn't for a moment think what she should do now. Barbara was in a room somewhere, but she was to be kept overnight. Billy . . .

She heard the crackle of the hospital PA system. "Dr. MacIntyre. Emergency surgery. Dr. MacIntyre. Emergency . . ."

She must find a telephone and call Jake. She must call Jake and tell him about Billy.

6

ONE MORE HURDLE

Jake was editing the lead story (Violence erupted on the campus Wednesday when the club-swinging city police attacked . . .) when the telephone in his office rang. He slapped the sheets of copy down on the managing editor's desk. "Rusty, read it for the last three 'graphs."

The phone rang again and Jake ran lightly across the newsroom to his office and scooped up the telephone receiver. "Stuart here."

"Jake, Jake!"

He knew instantly who it was even though the voice was tear-sodden and held together by will alone.

"Suzie," he said violently, "what have they done to you?"

"It's not me," she cried. "It's Billy. Oh Jake, his eye is gone! The doctor pulled that shirt away from his face and, Jake, Billy's eye is gone!" And her voice rose and sharpened.

"Hold it, Suzie! Hold it."

She drew one deep breath after another in the stuffy phone booth. Then she cracked the door to let in antiseptic-laden air.

"Suzie, where are you?" he asked urgently.

"At the hospital," she said blankly. "I've been here ever since they cleared the Greenway. Barbara got hurt and I came with her. Billy was in the hallway with all the rest of the kids who hadn't been treated yet and he was trying to convince this boy that we shouldn't want revenge and then he sort of reached out for the wall and he fainted. Billy fainted! Annette tried to hold him up but she couldn't. And it made so much noise when he fell." She paused and said in a faraway voice, "And Jake, Billy was gray, dusty-gray like an alley cat's fur."

"Tell me all of it," he said grimly.

When she had finished, Jake was silent for a long moment. He couldn't push words past the thickness in his throat.

Suzie spoke first and her voice was high and shrill again. "What if he dies? He was so gray. Jake, he was so gray! When they wheeled him away, they were calling for another doctor to meet them in surgery. Right then. Right that moment."

"That's a good sign," Jake said quickly. "They wouldn't operate if he was dying. They wouldn't try if he didn't have a chance. That's good news that they're operating." His voice quickened, "Maybe they can do something for his eye. You know, maybe it just looked real bad, but . . ."

"No," she said quickly, her voice thin again,

"OK," he said quietly. "OK. But it's still good that they're operating."

"He was so gray."

"Loss of blood. Shock. But, Suzie, he's strong! Billy's as big and tough as a bull. He'll make it."

And his conviction carried to her and lifted her up and, for the first time, she dared to hope. "He *is* strong," she said eagerly.

"Yeah," he replied, but in his mind he was back on the Greenway, helping them load Billy into an ambulance. And he hadn't looked closely at that bandaged head because it made him sick to see so much blood, welling and spreading into that thick brown hair. He hadn't truly helped his friend. And now Billy lay with his face the dusty-gray of an alley cat's fur . . .

"Jake?"

He held tightly to the receiver. "Suzie, listen to me. They beat Billy down and he never raised his hand against anybody. Somebody's going to pay for it. And that somebody is Dean Gorman. He's to blame for Billy's eye just as surely as if he'd swung the club himself. And it's up to the *Gazette* to tell the kids about Billy. And it's up to you to write the story."

She sat on the narrow metal seat in the stuffy phone booth and listened and couldn't believe what he was asking.

When she made no response, he said sharply, "Suzie, you've got to pull yourself together. I know you've had a hell of a day. I know you're close to coming apart, but I want you to take one more hurdle for me. We need a story on Billy and there's no time for you to come to the office and write. I want you to give me a story now. Over the phone."

She rested her head against the sticky metal of the phone. How could he ask her to do this? Billy was her friend. How could she write a story about him as if he were just anybody?

"Suzie, we can't let them get away with what they did to Billy!"

She rubbed at her eyes. But Billy wouldn't feel like that, would he? Would Billy want her to take his injury and make it big, make it a thing to rally the kids against Dean Gorman?

"It's happened, Suzie, and people have a right to know! Billy's got friends. He's got more friends than anybody. And they have a right to know what happened to him."

Billy did have friends, she thought numbly. He was one of the most well-known seniors on the campus. What he did was news. What happened to him was news.

"I'll try, Jake," she said tiredly.

He was asking her to do one of the toughest things a reporter ever has to do—to sit in a phone booth and, under the pressure of a deadline, to spin a story out of her mind, dictating as she thought. And to do it when she was emotionally involved in the story and utterly exhausted.

Jake hunkered his shoulder up to hold the telephone receiver against his chin while turning his swivel chair toward his desk. He grabbed a sheet of copy paper and rolled it into his typewriter. He didn't doubt for a minute that Suzie would come through.

She sat tensely in the phone booth, her eyes squeezed shut. She gripped the receiver with both hands. Finally, slowly, with long pauses, she began dictating:

Big Billy Kessler, brown-bearded editor of the Wilderness Voice, lay unconscious Wednesday evening in the hallway of St. Catherine Hospital's Emergency Ward. When the attending physician removed a blood-encrusted bandage, a massive wound on the right side of Kessler's face was revealed. Where his right eye should have been was a pulpy mass of bloody flesh. Kessler was in emergency surgery at the *Gazette* press time and his condition was not known. A humanities major from St. Louis, Mo., Kessler is a familiar political figure on the university campus. He edits the underground newspaper which opposes the Indochina war and supports a peaceful reordering of society's values in the United States. On Wednesday afternoon during the student confrontation with police power on the Greenway, Kessler attempted to approach the club-armed police. His hands empty, open and outstretched, Kessler walked . . .

Suzie dictated and paused, dictated and paused. Jake, his broad face intent, typed as she talked. The typewriter keys flicked out like a lizard's tongue, swift and pointed and accurate.

When she had finished the story, from Billy's fateful walk toward the police line to his determined stand in the hospital hallway, Jake read it back to her. She pushed her mind to this final effort, making a change in the third 'graph and redoing the last sentence. And then she sat in the phone booth and felt too tired even to hold the receiver.

"It's a good story, Suzie. A fine story."

She heard the words, but they couldn't reach her. "Thank you," she said emptily.

He frowned and tried again. "Suzie, we couldn't stand by and let somebody get hurt like Billy was and not do something about it! This is what the *Gazette* is supposed to do."

"I hope so," she said quietly.

"I know so," he said emphatically. "Now listen, you pick yourself up and come on over here. As soon as the *Gazette* goes to press, I'll take you home. OK?"

"OK, Jake. I'll come."

But after she hung up the receiver, she continued to sit in the narrow booth until, vaguely, she became aware that someone else was waiting to use the telephone. She pushed out the partially-open door and ducked past the waiting figure, murmuring, "Pardon me, please."

She walked very slowly down the hall. She didn't want to go to the *Gazette* office and be told what a good story she'd written on Billy. But she couldn't face that empty room at the dorm. And she wanted very much to be near Jake even though he wouldn't understand how she felt about the story on Billy. But it would help just to be near Jake.

She pushed through the double-doors at the end of the hall.

Martin Henley watched the doors close behind her. He had

waited by the telephone booth, impatient at first for its user to be finished, and then he had caught a few words and moved a little closer and listened as Suzie dictated her story on Billy.

Martin had listened, and his wild driving impatience to be gone from the hospital and back on the campus eased a little. He listened and thought and figured.

As he stepped into the phone booth, he checked his watch. Seven-twenty. Still plenty of time. He knew that the *Gazette* front page didn't lock up until eight o'clock.

He ran through his plan in his mind, then impatiently dialed the *Gazette* newsroom, holding the receiver awkwardly with his splinted hand.

Rusty Jacobs answered the phone.

"*Gazette* newsroom. Jacobs."

"Are you the right person to talk to about getting a story in the paper?" Martin asked hesitantly.

"That depends," Rusty said patiently. "What kind of story?"

"Well, listen, do you know a guy named Billy Kessler? You know, the one who puts out . . ."

Rusty interrupted, "Yes, yes. What about Billy?"

"Well, listen, I'm down here at St. Catherine's emergency . . ."

Rusty cut in again, not so patiently. "We already have the story on Billy. I appreciate . . ."

And this time, it was Martin's turn to interrupt. "You know all about the call for the rally on the Greenway tomorrow?"

Rusty's pause was short and intent and then he bristled with questions. "Rally? What rally? Who are you and what rally are you talking about?"

"I'm one of Billy's friends and everybody's all hung up, man, about what happened to Billy and we've put out the word to come to the Greenway tomorrow at 2 P.M. to show the university that they can't get away with it—and to show that we aren't scared."

Rusty was writing it all down and looking up at the round-faced wall clock (half an hour until the absolute deadline for page one and working it out in his mind where he'd put the little story. "Wait a minute," he said sharply, "what's your name?"

And Martin put just the right note of modesty in his voice. "Oh, that doesn't matter. I'm just one of Billy's friends and I thought as how you'd probably . . ." He broke off and turned his face away from the mouthpiece and called, "Oh, are they ready to see me, Sam? OK, I'll be right there." Then he spoke directly back to the receiver. "Listen, I have to run. They're going to X-ray my arm, but thanks a lot, fella." And he hung up.

And he knew as the line went dead that he had set it up. It couldn't possibly have played any better.

But he didn't spend too much time congratulating himself. One inning didn't make a ballgame. He dredged another dime up out of his pocket and dropped it in the slot and dialed and waited for an answer.

7

50 LBS. 1½ BY 8

Kathryn Ellington (heiress to the Ellington candy fortune, Ellington's Crispy Crunch Bars, and Ellington's Super-SweetStick) paced up and down her small, shabbily furnished living room.

She had been searching for Martin ever since the police had moved into the mass of kids. And she hadn't found him anywhere. She'd been to Boley Clinic and to St. Catherine's and, of course, to his apartment. Twice to his apartment.

She had given up, finally, to come home to her apartment and now that she was here she didn't know what to do!

This afternoon had proved everything she'd been told about the police and the university. It was a brutal conspiracy to destroy opposition to the system. Well, everyone would see the truth now! And now was the time to fight tyranny and destroy it.

She walked faster and faster, back and forth across the small room. The neon sign across the street flashed on and off, on and off, and each time the bronze-colored studs in the black footlocker near the window would glitter momentarily.

The bright flash caught her gaze and she slowed, then stopped and stared down at the footlocker. She leaned forward and her soft silky black hair swung about her face. She reached down and touched the slick surface of the footlocker.

All afternoon she had tried to find Martin because now was the time to strike. But if she had to, she could move forward on her own.

She knelt by the footlocker and unsnapped the hasps and lifted up the lid. The shiny yellow wooden box took up at least half the interior. Next to it sat a metal spool with bright orange line thickly wound about it. At the far end of the footlocker was a red circular tin container about four inches tall.

She leaned across the edge of the footlocker and pushed her fingers beneath the 50-pound yellow wooden box. Then, with a determined pull, she lifted the box up and balanced it on the corner of the chest. She rested for a moment, then more easily lowered the box to the floor.

The circular tin container she handled very gently, putting it on the coffee table across the room from the wooden box. The spool she grabbed up and thumped down right beside the box, then she sat down on the floor and read with great satisfaction the legend on the large yellow crate.

50 LBS. 1½ BY 8
DUPONT EXPLOSIVES
STRAIGHT DYNAMITE
60% STRENGTH

Of the many Kathryns—the tormented, the guilt-ridden, the angry—there was also a very capable and competent Kathryn with a knack and an instinct for putting things together with her hands. During her revolutionary instruction in Cuba, the instructor in the explosives class had singled her out as the best, the very best.

Nothing had ever pleased her so much.

She sat on the uneven humped grass mat in her living room and stared down at the yellow wooden case, but she was seeing again the stuccoed, bullet-pocked walls of their classroom and hearing again the soft liquid sound of Jaime's voice, "*La bonita señorita es el mejor de todos.*"

And she had been the best! She could prime and set a charge faster than anybody. And she was ice-steady when she lit the safety fuse, always waiting to see the brief flash of flame at the fuse end before she would turn to run. A lot of them hadn't had the guts for that.

It had been two summers ago when she had gone to Mexico on a holiday, then quietly left her hotel and walked to the Zocalo where a limousine had picked up her and four others and driven them to a private airstrip north of the District. Loud and boisterous with their sense of escape and adventure, they had boarded the DC-4 making its biweekly run to Cuba, carrying as usual an almost-full load of disillusioned and embittered young Americans, sure that their own version of the Golden Fleece must be somewhere just ahead.

Kathryn's six weeks in Cuba were the happiest she had ever spent. No one knew she was one of the Ellingtons. No one knew she was rich. Perhaps no one would have cared, but she didn't feel sure enough to test it. For six magic weeks she was one with a group. She lived in a dormitory, waking every morning to hurriedly pull on fatigues and rush downstairs to share in a communal breakfast of papaya and rolls and thick black coffee. Throughout the day she and her newfound friends attended classes in guerrilla warfare and revolutionary tactics and sabotage and explosives. She was accepted and even admired.

As she sat in her living room two years later and rubbed one hand lightly across the smooth varnished lid of the box, she could almost feel again the weight of the Cuban sun on her back and hear again the rumble of trucks along the rutted dirt road that passed by their compound.

Jaime had said she was the best. Now she would prove it. And she pushed up from the floor and stood, small and graceful, and a sure sense of success flowed through her.

The phone rang.

She looked at it blankly, absorbed in her thoughts. The strident ring sounded again. And again.

Irritably, she hurried to the phone and yanked up the receiver.

"Kathryn?"

"Martin!" she cried. "Where are you? I've been trying to find you for hours! Oh Martin,, listen I . . ."

He interrupted, certain of the importance of his words, his thoughts.

"Kathryn, can you pick me up? Now? At St. Catherine's?"

She looked across the room at the shiny yellow box and hesitated.

"Kathryn?" he asked impatiently.

"Yes," she said quickly, "I can come. Listen, Martin, I've . . ."

"Good. I'll be out in front on Chilton Street."

She stood in her living room and listened to the emptiness of a dead line. He had already hung up and she hadn't even had a chance to tell him. But she would hurry and tell him and he would see, too, that now was the time.

She did take time to put away the wooden box and the big spool and the small tin container. She snapped the hasps shut but she was thinking how soon she would be opening them again.

She locked the door behind her, twisting the knob to be sure, then turned and hurried down the stairs to the second floor, then along the uncarpeted hallway to the back stairs that would lead down to the fire exit and the alleyway.

It was dark and misty. The only light in the old bricked alley came from a street lamp at the cross street. Kathryn walked quickly past the uneven row of garbage pails and came to the little parking lot that served her apartment house.

She climbed into her old beat-up 1956 Chevrolet and tried to start it. The motor turned over and died. Dampness in the spark plugs, she decided. But she kept trying, very good-humoredly for her, because everything was going to be fine. Martin was found and now they would seize the moment, together.

Martin was striding up and down in the spreading light of a street lamp at the corner of Chilton and Maple. His cotton-white hair glistened in the bright white light. He walked with his head hunched forward, his Roman nose beaked above his sharply outthrust chin. His was a memorable face, the taut pale skin, the vivid blue eyes.

He heard the old car rattling up and swung to face it. As she pulled up by the sidewalk, he was hurrying toward the car. He pulled open the door and flung himself in the front seat and rasped, "Where the hell have you been? It's almost eight o'clock."

Kathryn's eager anticipation fell away.

He slammed the door shut. "Hurry up, will you? I want you to take me to the Union. Then I've got a bunch of things for you to do. I've got everything planned."

And Kathryn's hopes surged again. "Martin, listen, I've got . . ."

He was leaning forward in the seat as if by will alone he could make the old car go faster. He stared out through the windshield, his thick blond eyebrows knotted in thought. "I've got something rolling, Kathryn, that'll really put the squeeze on the university. If I can just get it started and get enough kids behind it, we'll raise so much hell they'll either have to boot ROTC or close the university." He paused and sat back in the seat. "Well have a list of demands," he said softly, almost to himself, "and if they won't meet them, we'll call a strike. And everybody'll come along with it because of Billy Kessler and Gorman and the whole bad deal on the Greenway."

He turned to look at Kathryn and his mouth curved in a satisfied smile. "We can't miss! All we have to do is emphasize how we oppose violence and rough stuff, how we want peace. We'll tell them everybody who hates violence must come to the Greenway tomorrow and show where he stands! And when we get them there, we'll lay it on 'em about what happened when Dean Gorman came with the cops. And look around and ask where the good dean is today? And ask what the program is . . ."

As he spun it out, Kathryn stopped listening. She drove jerkily, irritably, her face sullen. So Martin said there was to be no rough stuff, no violence. Well, rallies didn't make revolutions.

And she tried to say as much.

"But, look, Martin, so what?"

He stopped talking and stared at her.

She continued hurriedly. "I mean, so what will it prove to get everybody out to the Greenway again and maybe they'll call out the National Guard this time and everybody get pushed around? That doesn't do us any good."

He spread out his hands. "Don't you see, Kathryn? If they rough us up again, why, I'll be able to close this university down so tight a snail won't walk in a classroom." He leaned across the seat toward her. "And when they open it back up again, it will be run by the Committee of Five. Or it won't ever open."

"The Committee of Five?"

He smiled and said dreamily, "Yeah, me and four other guys." His smile broadened to a laugh, then, abruptly, he was serious again. "No, I mean it. It's going to happen here—and it will set a pattern that will sweep across the country. Universities will be student run." He arched a sardonic eyebrow. "The faculty will run scared. It will make them all nervous when we strike. Then we'll arrange some 'incidents' and pretty soon they'll be crying for the university to reopen."

Kathryn mulled over the idea of 'incidents' and decided, as she pulled up in front of the Union, to do it Martin's way, at least for now. And if they maneuvered a strike tomorrow, then perhaps that would be the time to urge Martin on to greater ventures.

So she asked very equably, "What do you want me to do?"

He glanced down at his watch. Five minutes to eight. It would be better, lots better, if he made it to the chamber before the session began, but it was important that Kathryn get it right. It was very important, almost as important as what he was going to do. So he took the time to make sure she understood what he wanted.

"Go to my place and call some of the kids. Get Bob Prosser and Walt Morey and Ralph Holcomb to come help. Then run off at least a couple of thousand handouts." He thrust a crumpled sheet of paper at her. "Here's the information. When you get 'em run off, a couple of you spread 'em out over the campus. The others can be calling people. Call everybody you know. Get the word out that the biggest rally of all time will be tomorrow."

He opened the door and started to get out.

She called after him. "But what are you going to do, Martin?"

He was checking his watch and slamming the door behind him. It was just a couple of minutes before eight. He broke into a run even though each pounding step sent a shock of pain through his splinted fingers. He didn't hear Kathryn. His mind was already a world away from Kathryn. He was planning and figuring and scheming—and hoping.

8

INVITATION TO DANGER

When the first ambulances had arrived that afternoon at the Greenway, the *ooo-wah* caterwaul of their sirens had brought at least a couple of dozen students to the windows of Gilbertson Memorial Library. What those students had seen and what they were told, as many of them hurried down to help, accounted for the first great wave of information that washed across the campus.

The uninjured students who went back to their dorms or trickled into the Union or the Boardman Street shopping area fed the swell. News of the confrontation spread far and farther.

The first film clips flashed across the state on the five o'clock news.

By seven o'clock Wednesday night, the news had even reached the University Observatory and Dr. Peter Porter, chairman of the astronomy department. A graduate student ran excitedly up the narrow steps to the telescope.

"Dr. Porter, sir, a riot! They say some students were killed and about fifty injured on the Greenway this afternoon. They say blood ran in the streets!"

Dr. Porter turned and stared at his assistant for a long moment. Then the stoop-shouldered astronomer shook his head. "My, you wouldn't think it of Greenlanders! They always seemed a most peaceable people to me." And he turned back to the telescope and began again to make notations in his notebook. The graduate assistant opened his mouth to speak, then shrugged and turned away.

The stories were wild and grew wilder. Three students dead. Four. Five. At least a dozen cops hurt. Somebody was seen carrying a rifle. Better be armed and prepared. The National Guard was coming! And bringing tanks!

It was talked about in the dorms, at the movies, in the head shops, in the back seats of cars, around pool tables, in taverns, in private homes, and boardinghouses.

By eight o'clock Wednesday evening, everybody knew.

And that made it so much easier for Martin Henley. When he came running down the hall to push open the ornate carved door (donated from the private collection of an alumnus and former U.S. Senator) that graced the entrance to the University Student Senate Chamber, everybody looked at his bandaged hand and his grass-stained slacks and they knew he had been on the Greenway.

The student senators, beginning to mill toward their seats to prepare for the opening of the weekly session, had been talking about the confrontation, arguing, speculating, imagining.

Martin paused just inside the door. Each student senator had his own small desk and the desks were arranged according to colleges. Each college had the number of senators proportionate to its enrollment. Beyond the orderly rows of desks was a wooden tier of seats for spectators.

Martin ran a hand disarmingly through his thick white-blond hair and looked about as if uncertain how to proceed. Then, with a gesture of relief, he raised a hand in greeting and walked toward Charley Sinclair, the president of the Student Senate.

"I don't know if you remember me," Martin began artlessly, "I'm . . ."

"Of course I remember you, Martin," Charley replied heartily. "Government 309, wasn't it? Professor Baker."

Martin nodded. "That's right."

He took Charley's outstretched hand and they shook hands, heartily.

"What can I do for you, Martin? We're about to get underway." He paused, then added, "The Student Senate, you know."

"Yeah, that's why I came," Martin said quickly. "I was down at St. Catherine's and I felt like I had to tell somebody who counted and I thought about you and then I remembered it was the night for the Senate to meet and so I came." He spread out his hands. "I don't know if anybody wants to hear me, but you ought to know what's happened." He paused and looked at the circle of faces around him. "Because you people help run the campus and you ought to know."

Charley, very much someone who counted, stood up to his full six feet two inches and said importantly, "Of course as student senators we are all vitally interested in gathering information about what happened today on the Greenway and I know that everyone will welcome the opportunity to have a firsthand report."

And very shortly, Charley had called the Senate into session and Martin was standing behind the lectern.

He told the story of what had happened on the Greenway very well and the silence was intense and absolute as he described Billy's openhanded approach to the line of policemen and his feelings as he watched the big senior fall beneath the blows of the clubs.

"That's why I came tonight. To tell you about Billy Kessler." He paused and his face tensed as he tried to explain. "Because you can do something about it. I can't do anything to show the university how the kids feel about Billy. You know who I am? I'm head of the Students for a Free Society. You know how many members my group has? Six. Counting me. So it doesn't make any difference what I do or say. But that's not true of the Student Senate."

Doris Casteel, a junior from the College of Law, flapped her hand up and down. Martin hesitated, but he knew he'd better recognize her.

She stood, tall and skinny and totally unimpressed. "Are we to believe, Martin, that you are informing us out of the goodness of your heart? I mean, is there really nothing in it for you, such as asking the Senate to endorse the anti-ROTC rally?" She paused and looked hard-eyed at her fellow senators. "I want to make my position clear. I regret injury to anyone but I cannot condone and will certainly not approve the actions of students who try to disrupt a university function, to wit, the ROTC drill." And she sat down amid nods of approval by quite a few of the senators.

Martin shook his head emphatically. "I wouldn't even think of asking the Student Senate to oppose ROTC. I know there are many of you who disagree with me politically. But I'm not here as a political person and I'm not asking for political support."

He paused and looked down. "In fact, I'm not asking anybody for anything. I'm just making a report." He rubbed his left arm, then said, "It does seem to me like the Student Senate should take some sort of stand about people being hurt on the campus. But that's up to the senators." Then he continued very quickly, "I do know that a lot of the kids down at St. Catherine's, the ones waiting in the hall to be treated, they were all pretty upset about Billy Kessler and there was a lot of talk about everybody coming to the Greenway at two tomorrow afternoon to show that they were opposed to police brutality. To kind of prove to the university that they couldn't be intimidated."

He stared somber-faced at the senators. "I know that I'm going to be there." He held up his splinted hand. "I have to go."

Suzie Torres huddled in Jake's swivel chair and stared out through the plate glass partition of his office into the empty *Gazette* newsroom. Jake and Rusty were downstairs, reading proof on page one.

Wearily, she looked up at the round-faced clock on the newsroom wall. Ten-fifty. Ten minutes until eleven o'clock and the press run. Then they could get out of here.

It was the first time she had ever wanted to be gone from the newsroom. But tonight she couldn't accept the way the *Gazette* went on no matter what. With Billy deep under anesthetic in an operating room, the newspaper continued on its impersonal way, spinning out the news of his injury as if he were only a name.

Suzie pushed the chair back from the desk and stood and opened Jake's door and paced out into the newsroom. She wanted to go home.

Suddenly the building seemed to rumble beneath her feet. The press run had begun. She watched the door that led to the backshop stairs and, expectedly, it opened in only a moment. Jake and Rusty walked slowly into the newsroom. Each carried a copy of the *Gazette*. Each read the front page. They stood, just inside the door, immersed in the magic of their creation.

"Damn," Rusty muttered. "Two graphs transposed in the wrap-up of eyewitnesses."

"Oh well," Jake said quickly, "it's very clean, all things considered. I only spot two typos and that's amazing with so much late copy."

"Yeah," Rusty said grudgingly, but underneath it, he was pleased. Page one looked good and it had been a total remake. "Yeah, it's all right."

Suzie had drawn even with them now. She stood and looked at them, appalled. Jake looked up and, mistaking her expression, said, "Hey, I'm sorry. Here's a copy for you." And he handed her a tabloid, then quickly turned back to study his copy.

She took it with an almost physical feeling of revulsion. The huge black head on the lead story seemed to leap out at her. Then her glance dropped to Jake's editorial, set indented so that extra white space would catch the reader's eye. She saw, briefly, her own bylined story on Billy.

Then her eyes were drawn and held by a boxed boldfaced announcement. And she looked at it with sharp dismay. It was she who had answered the phone about an hour ago and taken the information, then typed it up and given it to Rusty. It hadn't seemed such a terribly important thing then. She had given it to Rusty and he'd checked the time and said they'd just make it to put in a little last-minute bulletin.

But now, she looked at that black, black type and she saw it as an invitation to danger—and it was she who had written it.

She read it again:

The Student Senate voted Wednesday night 71 to 14 in favor of a resolution approving a rally of students on the Greenway at 2 P.M. Thursday to protest police brutality.

She stared down at the boxed bulletin, and knew that the

small square caught the eye quicker than the big headlines. The late twentieth-century mind is trained to scent disaster in last-minute boldfaced bulletins and so the eye darts immediately to the handful of black lines. What has happened? What is going to happen?

She put the paper down on the copy desk, but she couldn't blot its image from her mind.

Nobody should have planned another rally so soon! And even if they planned it, the *Gazette* shouldn't have printed it.

But, even as she thought it, she knew she wasn't being fair to the *Gazette.* It had to print the news, didn't it? But was it news until it was printed? Wasn't it the *Gazette*, offering up those black lines, that made it news?

She sighed and rubbed her eyes. She was so tired. Too tired to work it out. She only knew that when she looked at that small black box of type, she felt the same sense of wrong-ness that had overwhelmed her one afternoon when she had looked out on a sky turned purple with a hint of green. The rain had come, a driving slanting rain and, abruptly, the high whine of a wind gone mad, the jet-shrill scream of a tornado.

She picked up the *Gazette* and stared again at the page, then folded the tabloid and folded it again. She was just tired. It wasn't that big a thing. If she could just get out of there, everything would be better. She looked at Jake. He was still reading the *Gazette.*

"I have to go," she said abruptly. "I have to leave now, Jake."

Jake's head jerked up and he stared at her in surprise. Then, as she brushed past him on her way to the wide doorway, he said hurriedly, "Hey, Rusty, will you do the lockup?"

"Sure," the managing editor replied. He looked after Suzie, his face sympathetic and friendly. "She's pretty tired, huh?"

"Yeah," Jake said uncertainly, "I guess so." He yanked his jacket down from a peg. As he pulled it on and hurried after

Suzie, he called back to Rusty, "I'll hit Larsen's news conference in the morning."

Suzie was out of the double-door and halfway down the hall. Jake quickened his pace. "Hey Suzie, wait a minute. What's the matter?"

She didn't answer. She reached the top of the stairs and clattered down them. But she had to stop at the bottom of the steps in front of the narrow metal door, locked for the night.

Frowning, Jake pulled out his keys, unlocked the door and held it open for her. As she stepped out into the damply-cold October night, he locked the door behind them, then turned to follow her. He wouldn't have been surprised if she had been gone. But she waited, her back to him, in the deep pool of darkness by the side of the honeysuckle hedge.

He walked slowly to her and gently touched her arm. "Sue, why did you run away from me?"

He felt her deep shuddering sigh. She pressed her face into her hands. His touch shifted into a grip and he pulled her around and into his arms. She clung to him, her face hard against his shoulder.

Her voice was muffled. "It seems so wrong. To get a byline because Billy got hurt. To write another story asking everybody to come to the Greenway again. And you and Rusty looking at that page—and loving it! And all those kids hurt!"

He held her tightly, so tightly. In his mind he could see the Greenway and the line of policemen flailing at the kids. He could see bright spurts of blood, thick and shiny in the bright fall sunlight. He could hear the screams and shouts and the solid thuds. Again he could feel sickness inside himself, the swirl of nausea in his mouth and throat.

"You can be proud of a good job," he said haltingly, "even when the story breaks your heart." He paused, then said determinedly, "And you can't run away from a story—ever. It's your job to write so that people can know."

He cupped her chin in his hand and gently raised her face. "You have to do your job, Suzie. And you shouldn't be ashamed of that byline. It doesn't mean that you don't care."

He could scarcely see her face in the darkness but he could feel the warmth of the tears slipping down her cheeks.

He begged then, tears in his own voice, "Please, Sue baby, don't cry. Don't cry, honey. I'm here. It will be all right. Sue, honey, it will be all right." And his arms closed around her again and he bent his face until his lips found hers.

9

AH, THE GOOD OLD DAYS

President Larsen walked briskly. He always walked briskly. Long ago he had decided that all human beings were cold in wintertime but that hunching did not generate warmth and the upright homo sapiens was clearly more full of grace than those contorted like corkscrews. So he walked as tall as his five foot seven inches would allow and his arms swung freely at his sides and he breathed deeply of the damply cold night air.

He walked and relished the fresh night air and the fleeting glimpses of the fog that nestled in the low spots and shone like spun silver in the lights of passing cars.

He had to make a decision.

The meeting in his office had not been scheduled for decision making. He had called together his deans and vice-presidents so that the faculty and administration together could consider what had brought violence to the campus. But the telephone call at 9:57 from Dr. McGown, faculty sponsor of the Student Senate, changed the complexion of the gathering. The knowledge that the Student Senate had voted approval of a protest rally scheduled for tomorrow on the Greenway turned the meeting upside down.

Argument raged. What should be the university's posture? Opposition? Cooperation?

It was Vice-President Lucius Walters (Research and Development) who triggered an emotional storm.

"There's only one responsible answer," Walters trumpeted. "You must call in the National Guard."

Dean Abernathy's hands vibrated like fish fins as he declared, "That would be tantamount to declaring war on the students."

Vice-President Walters retorted, "We can't stand idly by and see the university burned to the ground!"

When Dean Abernathy raised his hands to heaven and implored to be shown the buildings in flames, Vice-President Walters cried, "It will come to that. The radicals are determined upon the university's destruction. It is our duty to protect the campus."

"Property instead of lives?" Dean Abernathy demanded.

"Property *and* lives," Vice-President Walters thundered. He glared around the table and his gaze locked on Dean Gorman. "Don't you agree, sir?"

Dean Gorman was not in a mood to agree with anybody about anything. It rankled him that apparently almost everyone seemed to hold him personally responsible for the whole mess! He looked at Vice-President Walters, frowned, and said irritably, "I think it's a toss-up. If you call the Guard, there'll be trouble. If you don't call the Guard, there'll be trouble." He thought about it a little harder, then said grudgingly, because he was an honest man in his own eyes, "Since it'll probably go to hell either way, I don't think I'd call the Guard."

"Who will protect innocent students from the onslaught of violence?" Vice-President Walters demanded.

"There are no innocent students," Dean Gorman responded bitterly.

"I say now," began Dean Abernathy.

"Gentlemen," President Larsen said quietly, "it is getting on toward eleven o'clock. I suggest we wait and gauge the temper of the campus in the morning."

"If you don't have the Guard here before those people gather on the Greenway tomorrow, you invite the ruin of the university," Vice-President Walters intoned grimly.

President Larsen straightened the papers on the table before him.

"Perhaps," he said quietly. "Perhaps not."

He pushed back his chair and stood and said firmly, "If it is convenient to you, I will hope to see all of you here at ten in the morning. I want to thank each of you for coming tonight." He paused. "With God's grace we shall hope to see our way through tomorrow without violence."

But as he walked through the cold damp night, reviewing in his mind the people and prejudices and passions that had struggled for primacy in his office, he felt very discouraged. They were all good men according to their own lights. Most of them, perhaps all of them, meant well. But there was no agreement among them.

That was not terribly important insofar as reaching a decision. He would make the decision. That was why he headed the university. To make the decisions. As a sign on Harry Truman's desk had proclaimed in other grave days, "The buck stops here." President Larsen understood that motto.

The difficulty was not in making a decision. The difficulty was in making a decision in such a fashion that the deans and vice-presidents would support it. They need not agree with it but they must support it or the stuffing would seep out of the university.

And he was very worried about what might happen on the Greenway tomorrow. He did owe a measure of protection to the students who would gather there, but he must at all costs avoid the appearance of power massed against students. It was going to be difficult.

What kind of students would rally on the Greenway tomorrow? What would be in their hearts?

He walked on through the night, his shoes clipping a quick, steady beat on the sidewalk. He looked ahead and saw with pleasure the luminous halos around the fog-wreathed street lamps. In the darkness near Pulitzer Hall, his stride checked for an instant. What was that odd shadow? Then the rhythm of his walk picked up again and a broad smile lighted his face.

How reassuring. Some things at least didn't change. Boys still kissed girls in campus shadows. For an instant, President Larsen felt quite relaxed. He was back again on the campus of long ago when grades and girls and parties had been big and the world beyond the campus a shadow play with little substance or meaning.

And for just a flicker of time, he wished that things were the way they used to be. Ah, the good old days, as the emcee would nostalgically sigh when the old film clips flickered to life. For just a moment, President Larsen longed for those days, for the orderly world with its dorm curfews and occasional scandals (Sally Cantrell didn't make it in and they fixed a dummy in her bed and her roommate opened the fire escape just before dawn and they got away with it!), and its beer busts and hazing (they dropped Tom Jones six miles out of town on a country road without his pants!), and its naive earnestness (gee, Procter and Gamble is interviewing in Grainger Hall today).

But as he neared the Architecture Building, he brushed the futile wish away, much as he would discard junk mail or an outdated newspaper. He must be getting old, he decided wryly. The compulsion to resist change is common to all men but especially to aging men. Therein, of course, lay the seeds of much of the discord in America today.

But how could he forget, even for an instant? His mind, the trained mind of a classicist, swung back to Heraclitus, who put it so well for all time: There is nothing permanent except change.

If a student learned only this, he was well equipped for life.

President Larsen pondered change. He had changed. The campus had changed. It was only to be expected that students had changed.

He looked up. Ahead of him loomed the Architecture Building, a marvelous example of change, a skyscraper taking its place among the ivy-sheathed halls on the campus. Just past the multi-storied building, spangled by the occasional lighted office, the hill and street sloped down. President Larsen's steps slowed as he saw the thick pool of fog at the base of the street. When he reached the thick patch and fog began to swirl about him, he saw that he could dimly make out a pale glow ahead that would mark a street lamp and the beginning of the Greenway, so he plunged ahead.

Then, in the unexpected fashion of fogs, the mist thinned and President Larsen could see a kneeling figure at the street corner some twenty feet ahead.

At almost the same moment, the young man heard footsteps and looked back over his shoulder. Abruptly, he scrambled to his feet, grabbed at something, then ran.

Instinctively, Larsen pounded after him. He was a classicist by trade, a long-distance runner for pleasure.

His body responded instantly to the suggestion of stealth in the hunched figure and the implication of guilt in the startled run.

Larsen covered the twenty feet to the corner in seconds, but the running figure was hidden in the thick fog that swathed the Greenway. Larsen stopped and listened, but fog distorts sound and distance. It would be a pointless pursuit.

Instead, he looked down to see what his startled quarry had been doing.

The letters were raggedly painted. They sprawled across the sidewalk.

STRIKE!

Beyond the painted word, he saw a dumped-over paint can that the young man had upset when he scrambled to his feet. In the path of the slowly spreading paint was a paper sack.

Larsen stepped over the paint stain and looked inside the sack, then gingerly picked it up and pulled out the top sheet from a pile of mimeographed papers.

He read it expressionlessly.

BOOT ROTC!
CAN GORMAN!
OR STRIKE!
REMEMBER WHAT THEY DID TO BILLY KESSLER!
COME TO THE GREENWAY 2 P.M. THURSDAY
LET'S TELL THEM SO THEY HEAR. YOU KNOW WHAT THEY DID.
YOU KNOW WHO DID IT. DON'T LET THEM THINK THEY'RE
GETTING AWAY WITH IT.
BOOT ROTC!
CAN GORMAN!
OR STRIKE!

He tucked the sack under his arm and stared down at the

spreading paint, but somehow it wasn't either the painted word or the printed message that made the night seem suddenly colder, inimical. It was the way the street light shone down on that still softly spreading paint.

It was red paint, bright red paint. In the light it curled across the sidewalk as thickly and slowly as blood.

When he walked slowly on, he no longer looked at the delicate nimbuses of light that graced his way.

He walked and his face was grave. He was not a superstitious man, but he wondered inside himself, which was the omen? The kiss in the shadows or the blood-red splash on the sidewalk?

10

PEOPLE, NOT SLOGANS

The wind veered to the north during the night. By dawn it was gusting up to 45 miles an hour, a cold wet penetrating wind that rattled the old wooden window frames in Jake's garage apartment and bulled its way in between cracks and crevices to chill the room.

The cold woke Jake. His eyes still tightly shut, he pawed sleepily for his blanket, then realized vaguely that he was not only cold but uncomfortable. He was sleeping on an incline and his pillow itched and the blanket was too short and . . .

He was on the couch and the blanket was too short because it was really his coat and a beach towel! Abruptly, he was fully awake and swinging his legs around to sit up on the rumpled couch and look across the room at Suzie asleep in his bed.

He stood and walked softly across the room to stand beside the bed.

She slept face down, her head burrowed into the pillow, one hand tightly clutching the edge of the pillowcase. He could see the right side of her face and the streak of dried tears still on her smooth dark cheek. He reached out hesitantly to gently touch her black hair.

She stirred, then pushed deeper into the pillow and slept on.

He went around the bed and over to the closet and pulled down a thick soft quilt and returned to spread it over the sleeping girl. Then he stood, his head thrust forward in its characteristic way, his gray eyes serious and thoughtful.

Last night Suzie had clung to him and he had known that she dreaded the return to her empty room. He had brought her home with him and laughed and teased and fixed hot chocolate and been enormously pleased when she managed a wan smile. She had plummeted into sleep, the sleep of exhaustion and escape. He pushed away the impulse to wake her. Let her sleep while she could. Let her be free of yesterday as long as she might.

Instead, he leaned over the bed and tucked the quilt around her shoulders. A smile flicked in his mind at the unaccustomed gentleness of his broad, stubby hands.

Then, briskly but quietly, he started the morning, lighting the small gas stove, shaving, dressing, plugging in the coffeepot.

And still Suzie slept.

The room was warming now. The coffee perked and its fragrance spread over the room. Jake poured the coffee into a thermos, then reached up into the wooden cabinet for two cups and saucers. When he turned to set them on the small kitchen table, he saw Suzie gravely watching him.

He put the cups down then strode across the room, and his blunt face was happy and his broad mouth was spread in a smile.

"I know it's the coffee that woke you, but I'll pretend it's hunger for my company."

She smiled at him, then sat up. "Both," she said diplomatically.

She stretched out her hands. "Jake, you're very nice to let me stay and take your bed away and then even to fix breakfast the next morning."

"Lady, I'd be glad to have you stay any time at all."

She swung off the bed and stood. Even in his floppy too-big pajamas she was lovely, her dark eyes a vibrant brown, her tousled hair shining black, her soft skin a creamy brown.

Then she looked up at him, her brown eyes gravely questioning.

And he said quietly, "And I do mean it."

She looked at him, then put up her hands to frame his broad solid face. "Thank you, Jake." She stood on tiptoe and lightly kissed him and said quickly, "If you'll pour me a cup of coffee, I'll hurry and dress."

He whistled cheerfully while she was in the bathroom and when she came out, once again in the leather skirt and bolero jacket and pale yellow blouse she'd worn yesterday, he said, "I really think I like you better in pajamas—my pajamas."

It was a fun breakfast even though the best the larder could muster was a box of graham crackers. But the coffee was excellent and the company even better.

It was Jake who finally broke the spell. He finished his second cup of coffee, then looked down at his watch and Suzie knew that gesture signaled the end of that small piece of charmed time.

He was pushing back his chair, his blunt face already creasing in thought. "Listen, Suzie, do you want me to drop you off at the dorm?" He looked at his watch again. "It's five to eight. I want to stop off at the *Gazette* before I go to Larsen's conference. I want to be ready for him."

She looked up, puzzled. "Ready for him?"

"Yeah," Jake said emphatically. "Larsen may think he's going to palm some slick statement off on us, but he's wrong. Because

I've got the questions and I'm going to ask them and if he tries to flimflam us, it will have to happen in front of God and everybody."

Suzie frowned. "Jake, I think President Larsen is a good man. I mean, I don't think he would lie about anything. He'll try to do what he thinks is best for the university."

Jake's big head hunched forward. "We've gone beyond playing things so the university will look good. That doesn't matter any more. What matters is what the university did to the kids."

She was standing now, too, and she reached out toward him.

"Jake, the university didn't do anything to anybody! It was Dean Gorman and the police!"

His jaw jutted out and he turned away from her outstretched hand to reach for his jacket. "I'm talking about ultimate responsibility," he said harshly. "Dean Gorman called out the cops, but he did it because the university won't tolerate opposition to ROTC." He shrugged into his jacket and zipped it up. "Coming?"

She gathered up the coffee cups and the box of graham crackers. "No," she said quietly. "I'll straighten things up a bit, then walk. I'm not in any hurry this morning."

When he was gone, the door slamming behind him, she stood by the table, holding the cups, wanting to call him back. But she didn't want the angry, vengeful Jake. She wanted the kind and gentle and generous Jake.

Eben Petrowski nodded good morning to Mrs. Bassett, who ladled out the scrambled eggs behind the cafeteria counter every morning except Sundays. He had been eating his breakfast in the Union for three years now, except during the two weeks it was closed in August for the annual repainting of the beige walls. Mrs. Bassett had been in charge of the bacon and sausage and eggs for almost eighteen years. She greeted Petrowski as one of her regulars.

"Good morning, Chief. The weather's turned on us, hasn't it."

"Looks like. But it's time for a little winter. Believe I'll have sausage this morning, Mrs. Bassett."

It was a cheerful beginning to his day, this customary exchange with Mrs. Bassett. For a lonely man, it was nice to have his breakfast handed to him with a smile.

He moved his tray slowly along the rails. There was no need to hurry. The line was short this early in the morning.

He carried his tray to one of his favorite tables at the back of the room where French windows opened out onto a red-bricked patio with a goldfish pond in the center and low marble benches around it.

This morning, wind-driven rain slatted into the pond. Thick black clouds closed up the sky. But Chief Petrowski watched the big globules of water splatter and spread against the glass and loved every cold wet particle of rain that fell. If the weather stayed like this or, even better, turned colder, there wouldn't be many kids on the Greenway this afternoon. And the fewer the kids, the less likelihood of somebody's getting hurt. In Petrowski's view, the weather was the first nice thing that had happened since yesterday afternoon.

He set his breakfast out—sausage, scrambled eggs, toast, jelly, and coffee. Then he neatly put the silverware in place—knife and spoon to the right, fork and napkin to the left of his plate. That was the way Mae had always fixed his breakfast, everything in place, the hot things hot, the cold things cold.

He reached over and put the tray on the webbed stand, then sat down. Somehow it was always tough at breakfast. Maybe it was because Mae had always tried so hard to fix it just the way he wanted it. But most of all he missed her loving smile and the eager way she watched him eat when it was something new and different, like pecans and grated oranges sprinkled on top of pancakes.

There hadn't been any kids. Just the two of them and Mae always so patient when he was gone on sea duty. She had looked forward so much to his retirement and the two of them always being together. Retirement had been only half a year away when the sharp pain had come, low in her back, and before three months passed, Mae was dead.

He stared blankly out the French windows, then abruptly grabbed up a copy of the *Gazette* that some earlier breakfaster had left on the table. Petrowski poured his coffee, added two teaspoons of sugar, then looked at the tabloid's front page.

His right hand curved around the coffee cup, but he didn't pick it up. Instead, he looked at each headline on the page—and the overall effect stunned him.

The lead story headline was five columns wide:

COPS SLAM KIDS

In the middle of that lead story, a boldface box announced the Thursday rally on the Greenway.

A two-column head on Billy Kessler ran to the left of the lead story. Then the eyes were pulled down the page to Jake's editorial, set in 10-point body type, big enough and leaded with enough white space to make it distinctively different from the surrounding stories.

The chief's eyes ran down the editorial, ". . . the pablum, the pitch, the reasoning smile—and then the club . . . the kids sang . . . the cops rioted . . . the hell you say!"

Petrowski crumpled the paper in his hands. He drank his coffee, lukewarm now, in one swift gulp. Then, tamping down his anger, he spread the paper out again. He ate and methodically read every word. When his plate was empty, he sat and stared somberly at the front page of the *Gazette.*

He wasn't sure it was his place to do what he intended to do. And he didn't know if it would help. But it might. And that was reason enough.

So when he rose to go, a tall lean man with a wrinkled, reddish face, he moved as quickly but not as confidently as usual. He was heading out in uncharted waters. He knew his destination, of course, because the campus was his territory, his responsibility. He knew which buildings muggers lurked near. He knew which basements pot salesmen favored. He knew the entrances and the exits and the underground steam tunnels. He knew the campus as a cop, not a student.

And when he pushed out through the side door of the cafeteria, forcing the door out against the wind, he checked the parking lot with a cop's eye. That black '56 Ford had been there for at least three days. Make a note to have Alan check the registration and haul it in.

He was coming out of the back of the Union. He turned and walked to the sidewalk that paralleled Hurlburt and turned south. He walked fast, the wind hard at his back. He passed the dignified red-bricked Graduate College and the white stone Engineering Hall, which sprawled the length of a block. Halfway down the next block, where it began to curve, he could see shabby Pulitzer Hall, a very plain red-brick box which dated back to the post-World War II building boom.

Petrowski's steps slowed when he was still a half block away. No lights shone from the windows. For the first time it occurred to him that he might find the building empty at this early hour. He stopped and frowned, then shoved his hands a little deeper in his raincoat pockets and walked briskly on.

At the front door of Pulitzer Hall, he almost turned away. The central hall was dark. He hesitated, then stepped inside, welcoming the respite from the sharp sting of the rain and the icy north wind. He stood for a moment in the dark entryway. Water dripped off his raincoat onto the floor. It was very quiet. He could hear the soft hiss of the steam radiators. Reaching out, he pulled down the light switch and a white-bowled overhead light glowed. He saw the stack of *Gazettes* on a small table near the door. On the wall to the left hung a room directory. He studied it, then started up the gray painted stone steps.

On the second floor, he saw the soft glow of light in the north wing. The *Gazette*'s wing. He hurried toward the light, pulling his copy of the morning paper out of his pocket.

He stopped at the open double-door of the newsroom to look curiously at the horseshoe-shaped copy desk and the rows of small desks with their assortment of typewriters and the long line of yellow oak filing cabinets and, to his right, the glass-paneled office that sat alone.

He watched with great interest the intent face of the stocky young man sitting at the yellow oak desk in the small office.

Then he walked slowly across the wooden floor to knock on the office door. Jake looked up. Recognizing his visitor, he rose and opened the door. "Chief Petrowski. What can I do for you, sir?"

The chief hesitated. "I don't really have any business coming here."

"Everybody's welcome in this office, Chief."

The tall lean man looked down and said slowly, "All right then, I'll ask you who is responsible for this." And he held up his wrinkled rain-spattered copy of the *Gazette*.

Jake stood a little straighter, hard-solid on his heels, chin up. "I am."

The chief nodded, then said quietly, "You're going to get somebody killed."

Jake stood very still for an instant, then his head jutted forward and he stepped a pace toward the bigger man.

"You came to the wrong office, Chief Petrowski."

The older man frowned. "You are Jake Stuart, the editor, aren't you?"

"Right. But you don't want my office. You want Dean Gorman's office."

Chief Petrowski's reddish face turned a deeper red, but his voice was as even and controlled as always. "No. I want you. I'm talking about what is going to happen, not what did happen." And his eyes fell to the front page.

Jake followed his glance. "So that's your pitch, that the *Gazette* is going to start trouble by reporting what happened." He shook his head. "That's putting the blame on the wrong horse." He looked sardonically at Petrowski. "You were there. Are you going to tell me those stories are wrong?"

The campus cop frowned. "Mr. Stuart, I'm not clever with words. I never have been. But I was on the Greenway and I know why there was trouble. It happened because Dean Gorman doesn't have any feel for people and because he hates the way kids are loose and easy." The man looked down again at the *Gazette*. "And even so, it might have gone OK if the cops hadn't been scared."

Jake stared at him for a long moment, then he laughed, a short derisive laugh.

Chief Petrowski said steadily, "That's right, son. They were scared. Don't you know a man gets scared when he thinks somebody's going to kill him?"

Jake rubbed the back of his neck, then asked abruptly, "Chief, are we talking about the same scene? I mean, who had the clubs?"

The tall man hunched his shoulders and shoved his hands down into his raincoat pockets. "A club won't help against a gun. And there've been too many bullets with cops' names on them the last couple of years. The odds are bad for cops lately. A cop answers an emergency call and a sniper's waiting in a grove of trees. He tries to break up a crowd and somebody is up on a roof with a rifle. So all the time a cop's neck aches because he's trying to brace against a bullet."

Petrowski stared down at the floor. "Of course, it doesn't do a man any good to brace against a bullet. Cops know this. But a man will do it anyway."

Jake's mouth twisted. "OK, so the cops were scared. I don't buy it myself. They didn't look scared. They looked big and tough and mean. But anyway, say they were scared. How does that add up to thirty-eight kids in the hospital?"

"Because the cops thought somebody had shot Captain Bristow. It was a pop bottle but it sounded loud when it smacked his head and blood spurted everywhere. And because they are trained to stay and fight even when somebody's shooting at them, they moved right into the crowd. You ought to remember, son, that they thought somebody had a gun and they moved forward anyway."

"My God," Jake said slowly, "next thing I know, you'll be calling for orchid leis to drape over the heads of our valorous dedicated policemen! Why, you think they did a swell job!"

"Dammit, no!" Petrowski exploded. "I didn't say that at all! I'm explaining what happened, why it happened. Look, kid, you're not the only person in the world who can see it's wrong for a bunch of people to get beaten up, but the reason why is important!"

"We agree on that," Jake retorted.

Petrowski held up the *Gazette*. "Look at this front page! It doesn't explain why the Greenway happened. Why, you read it and you think the cops deliberately knocked everybody around, that it was some kind of plot by the university!"

"It happened because the university is determined to keep ROTC no matter what happens," Jake said bullishly.

"No," Petrowski said loudly. "No. It's a lot simpler than that. It's because Dean Gorman is the kind of man he is and because somebody threw a pop bottle and because the cops were scared. And that's the story. It was a damn bad mistake but it wasn't a plot!"

Jake ran his hand through his thick brown hair, then said patiently, "Chief, don't you see that the important thing is that it is repression and it's all part of the Establishment resistance to change?"

The older man looked down at Jake's earnest face and he suddenly felt very tired. He sighed and said slowly, "No, son. It was people on the Greenway yesterday, not slogans. It wasn't the university and the police and the protesters. It was Dean Gorman and Martin Henley and Billy Kessler and me and you and a bunch of scared cops and a lot of kids."

He folded the *Gazette* and stuffed it in his pocket, then he looked right at Jake. "And it won't be what the administration or the police or the students do that will matter this afternoon. It will be what I do and what President Larsen does and what you do and what is done by a lot of people we don't even know about right now that will make the difference."

11

WHAT EVERYBODY'S SAYING

Suzie twisted the hot water knob and luxuriated in the increasing warmth. Shower water splattered over her, the heat pinkening her skin. Steam swirled in the stall. She closed her eyes and absorbed warmth. Slowly, slowly, the hot spears of water drove the chill out of her bones.

She had walked the eight blocks from Jake's apartment to her dorm, walked all the way with the wind hurling rain against her back. Her coat was sodden before she'd gone a block. Her boots squished and her feet ached with cold.

She had run the last block, to stumble breathless and wet and cold into the dorm foyer. Now she stood in her shower and she wanted to stay there forever and feel the heavy warmth of the water as it cascaded down her body.

So at first she tried to ignore the sharp penetrating voice.

"Suzie, is that you, Suzie?"

Suzie turned slowly around in the stall and the water rolled over her back and hips and ran in swift soft rivulets down her legs.

"Suzie? Suzie, they said downstairs that you'd come in. Suzie, this is Peggy. Aren't you about through showering?"

Suzie gave the cold knob a vicious twist, then turned it abruptly back again when the icy water struck her. The warmth returned but not the relaxed feeling of immersion. She gave up then and turned off the water, still trying to ignore the shrill voice beyond the glass door. She wondered irritably who in the hell Peggy thought was in the shower. Dustin Hoffman? But as she yanked open the door and stepped out on the green-tiled floor, she said only, "Yes, Peggy, it's me."

She pulled off her shower cap, then began to dry with a thick blue towel. Peggy leaned near the mirror over the make-up ledge, ostensibly applying eye shadow.

"Well, we certainly did miss you and Barbara last night! You didn't come in all night long!"

Suzie seesawed the towel across her back and said, "Hmm."

Peggy forgot her eye shadow long enough to lean perilously far to the right to peer into Suzie and Barbara's room. "Barbara?" When there was no answer, she turned her plump sensation-hungry face back toward Suzie. "And Barbara still hasn't come in! Whatever did you two do last night?"

Suzie was shrugging into her robe. "Barbara's in the hospital. We were on the Greenway yesterday and she got hurt."

Peggy trailed along behind Suzie as the slender dark-haired girl crossed into her room.

"Oh, we heard all about it on the news last night!" Peggy exclaimed. "And you were actually there! And then you spent the night at the hospital."

Suzie knew that Peggy was disappointed. It wasn't the hospital that she had envisioned. But almost immediately Peggy's spirits picked up because the Greenway was exciting news right now. She began to pull and press for details.

"Actually to be in a riot! Ooh, I'll bet it was scary."

Suzie slipped on her panties, then fastened her bra.

"It was obscene," she said shortly.

Peggy plopped down on Barbara's bed. "The hospital," she said thoughtfully. Her pudgy face crinkled in a frown. "Gee, is Barbara hurt bad?"

Suzie knew that in her own fashion Peggy actually did care how badly Barbara was injured even though it was her ferret-like instinct always to probe for information. Every fact she gathered was stored to be exchanged on the gossip's market, paying her way for a moment into an intimacy with others. So Suzie knew that when she answered she would be supplying Peggy with her chief commodity—information—and that soon almost everyone in the dormitory would know about Barbara and her injury.

Poor nice silly Barbara, so innocently proud of her soft fair skin and pretty face. What would it mean to her to be disfigured? How could she bear for everyone to know?

Suzie pulled her heavy brown tweed pants suit out of her closet and began to put it on. "Barbara'll probably get to come home this morning," she said evasively. "She has a cut on the side of her head but it will be all right."

Peggy wriggled excitedly. "So you were right there on the Greenway. Then you'll know." She jumped up and crossed to stand close to Suzie. "Is it true what everyone's saying?"

Suzie stepped back a pace and buttoned up her suit coat. "I don't know what everybody's saying."

"Everybody's saying that it was all deliberate, the whole thing!"

Suzie was reaching for her hairbrush. She paused to stare at Peggy. "Deliberate?"

"Yes," Peggy exclaimed. "It's all over the campus that the university planned the whole riot to make it look like ROTC was being persecuted! They say President Larsen is afraid the Research Institute will lose a bunch of Defense Department contracts if ROTC is kicked off the campus. And you know who's head of the Research Institute!"

Suzie shook her head.

A flicker of malicious delight glittered in Peggy's eyes. "Dr. Alan Fenner, President Larsen's brother-in-law!"

"That's absurd," Suzie retorted sharply. She picked up her hairbrush and began to brush her hair vigorously. "It's all absurd."

Peggy shrugged a little huffily. "I only know what everybody's saying."

Suzie crossed to Barbara's chest of drawers and began to lay out fresh clothes to take to the hospital.

"Who's everybody?"

Peggy shrugged again. "Oh, just everybody," she said vaguely. "Some kids called last night to tell the dorm about the rally today and somebody else heard about Dr. Fenner at the cafeteria this morning. It's all over campus. And somebody from Garrity Hall called Ann Hooker down on two and said it was a right-wing plot to get Billy Kessler."

Suzie shook her head. "That's not true, Peggy. It just didn't happen that way." She snapped the lid to Barbara's overnight case shut, pulled her own and her roommate's raincoats out of the closet, and turned to go.

Peggy caught her sleeve. "Suzie, you were there. What did happen?"

"Dean Gorman lost his temper and somebody threw a bottle and the cops overreacted," she said shortly. She pulled her arm free and started out the door. "I need to get these things to Barbara. I'll see you later, Peggy."

She was at the end of the hall, turning toward the stairs, when she heard Peggy's high sharp voice. "Kay, Barbara Murphy's in the hospital! She was hurt on the Greenway. And do you know what I've heard? Everybody's saying it was a deliberate attack . . ."

Suzie's lips thinned and she clattered hurriedly down the steps. She wasn't in any hurry to get back to the hospital, but she wanted to be as far as possible from the sound of Peggy's voice.

She was on the landing between the second floor and the lobby when she met Harriet Easton who was coming up.

Harriet, a tiny blond economics major, clutched Suzie's wrist with a birdlike hand. She held a copy of the *Gazette* and a sheet of blue paper in the other hand.

"I just read your story about Billy Kessler. Suzie, is it true that it was a right-wing attempt to silence Billy?"

"My story doesn't say that!"

Harriet shook her head impatiently. "No, no, I didn't mean that. But that's what everybody was saying at breakfast in Gallagher Cafeteria. Do you know if it's true?"

"No. No, I'm sure it's not. Harriet, it all just happened! Nobody planned any of it!"

Harriet thought about it for a moment. "That's very interesting. But I'm afraid nobody will believe it. Everybody's saying it was deliberate. And I understand that these are all over the campus." And she handed the blue sheet of paper to Suzie.

Suzie read it swiftly, BOOT ROTC! CAN GORMAN! OR STRIKE!

And Harriet said quietly, "I'll tell you, Suzie, everybody's upset. If President Larsen doesn't sack Gorman, I think the kids will strike!"

12

DON'T EVER FALL DOWN!

The hard hot glare of the strobe lights beat down on President Larsen. The brilliant white beams spotlighted the man and his desk. Sweat dampened the collar of his shirt and trickled down his back and chest, but he sat with ease and dignity, his hands resting lightly on the penciled sheets of his prepared text.

He didn't read the text. He looked levelly at the television camera and spoke soberly in his dry, slightly flat tenor voice, a small gray man in a big leather chair, and he was very impressive indeed.

". . . in sum, the violence on our campus occurred because of misunderstanding and misjudgment on the part of everyone involved."

He paused, took off his horn rim glasses, and said, "These mistakes will not happen again."

Folding the glasses, he dropped them into his coat pocket. "I feel confident that the university will survive this hour of travail and go forward stronger and wiser. All the university will gather this afternoon on the Greenway to reflect upon what occurred there yesterday. Classes will be dismissed so that all faculty members and students may attend."

He looked down at his gleaming desk top for a moment, then again faced the camera. "And perhaps we will take the opportunity to reflect upon the words of Plutarch in writing of Sertorius, an able but not brilliant general who yet had the wit to understand this fact: Perseverance is more prevailing than violence; and many things, which cannot be overcome when they are together, yield themselves up when taken little by little."

He waited a moment, then looked past the camera to the group of waiting newsmen. "Your questions, gentlemen."

Don Ryan, head of the state AP bureau, asked, "Do you expect trouble this afternoon?"

"No," President Larsen replied confidently.

"Why not?"

"Students and faculty will be gathering to show their antipathy to violence, Mr. Ryan. This is not a riot situation."

"Will you have cops laid on?" demanded Allie Fiske of the *Morning Herald.*

"No."

Betty Eberle of the state's largest daily said crisply, "The campus is flooded with handouts calling for a strike if you don't drop ROTC and fire Dean Gorman. How do you intend to respond?"

It was abruptly very still in the long room with its thick carpets and heavy drapes and row upon row of richly-bound volumes.

President Larsen said thoughtfully, "I plan to discuss the student demands at the rally. I would say now that I hope students see the futility of striking. It is the student who loses in such a situation. It is quite possible to disagree without closing up the shop."

"Mr. President."

President Larsen looked into the clear gray eyes of Jake Stuart.

"Yes, Mr. Stuart?"

"In your statement, Mr. President, you indicate that blame for the violence must be shared alike by administrators, students, and police."

President Larsen leaned forward a little and said clearly, "I did not speak in terms of blame, Mr. Stuart."

"Are you saying then," Jake demanded, "that it wasn't anybody's fault?"

"I am not apportioning fault. I intend to appoint a commission of faculty and students to explore what happened and to make recommendations."

Jake edged past the other reporters and walked up to stand squarely in front of President Larsen's desk.

The TV cameraman moved quickly but smoothly to the left so that he could get a side view of the president and the editor.

Jake hunched forward, his blocky body balanced on the balls of his feet. "Did Dean Gorman order the cops to move everybody off the Greenway, Mr. President?"

"Yes," President Larsen said shortly.

Jake stood immobile. The time stretched out and the answer bore the weight of the room.

Satisfaction flickered in Jake's eyes. He let the silence ride and expand to the last possible instant, then he asked sharply, "Are you going to fire Dean Gorman?"

President Larsen's eyes were cold and angry, but he spoke in such a controlled fashion that it took a moment for the words to jolt home to Jake.

"Mr. Stuart, you are much too young to remember the Army-McCarthy hearings in the 1950s, but your technique today is in the tradition of Senator McCarthy. I believe now, as I believed then, that demagoguery ultimately self-destructs."

Then the small ,gray man pushed back his chair, rose, and looked beyond Jake to the other newsmen. "Are there other questions?" When no one responded, he said quietly, "Good morning, gentlemen."

The reporters from the wire services and the state dailies began to amble out of the office. The TV newsman cased up his camera, then began to take down his lights.

Jake stood bullishly in front of President Larsen's desk. "You think I'm dumb!" he said angrily. "Hell, I know who McCarthy was! He persecuted people! I'm not doing that!"

"What were you trying to do to Dean Gorman—over statewide television?"

Jake said stubbornly, "It's his fault. And you're trying to let him get away with it."

President Larsen walked around his desk and stood by Jake.

"Look, son, I'm not trying to protect him; I'm trying to save the university. And at the least, I owe Dean Gorman judgment by a commission and not mob justice. And, too, why destroy him even if it was in part his fault?"

Jake frowned and started to speak, but the president continued. "Dean Gorman has spent his life in higher education. He made a mistake, but anybody can make a mistake."

"Billy Kessler's going to go through life with one eye," Jake said resentfully. "I think the dean's mistake was too big to gloss over. I think he's going to have to pay for this one.

"There is justice," President Larsen said quietly, "and there is justice tempered with mercy." He looked into Jake's hostile angry face and said, "My advice to you, young man, is to visit a turkey farm some day."

Jake frowned, not sure he had heard correctly.

"That's right," President Larsen said, "a turkey farm. Turkeys are big and powerful but very docile. They don't give any trouble to anyone. But when turkeys run, if one of them falls down, the other turkeys will trample him to death." The president stared levelly at Jake. "My advice to you, young man, if you choose to pursue vengeance in this life, is to be very careful never to fall down."

And with that he turned away and walked back behind his desk. He sat down and picked up a yellow legal pad and began to make notes in his small neat handwriting.

Jake would have followed but somehow President Larsen's secretary, Miss Scott, had moved between Jake and the desk. Miss Scott was tall and big-boned and she wore her hair in a truly awesome beehive. Her voice was quiet and modulated but somehow commanding.

"We have facilities in the anteroom for the press." And without actually touching him, she managed to turn him about and head him toward the door.

"Copies of President Larsen's statement are available on the first table to your right in the anteroom. And if there are any further questions, Mr. Putney, our director of public relations, will be delighted to help."

And Jake was standing outside the president's office, holding a copy of the statement and turning around in time to see the big wooden double-doors close.

His broad mouth twisted in a reluctant smile. The old she-devil had out-maneuvered him. Then the smile slipped away. He stared down at the Xeroxed statement and read it over once again, then shook his head. It slipped and slithered over all the important questions, like what about ROTC and what would be done about the dean.

Jake lifted his head and stared at the closed wooden doors.

And Larsen hadn't met Jake's questions head on. All he'd done was be very moral and prate on about how every man could make a mistake. But Dean Gorman was a big boy and big boys have to pay the piper. And besides, Jake thought bitterly, they'd sure lay it on a kid if he made that kind of mistake!

So Jake crumpled the statement in his hand and strode out of the anteroom, brushing past the group of reporters that had gathered around Tom Putney, Director of Public Relations.

Ryan of AP watched him go, then scrawled in his notes: student editor storms out of president's office after accusing president of shielding dean.

Then Ryan looked up at Putney and demanded pugnaciously, "Now, you can't be telling us that no provision has been made for trouble. That doesn't make sense. Give . . ."

Behind the closed doors of President Larsen's office, Miss Scott sat in a chair beside the desk, her stenographer's notebook in her lap, waiting. Her face was drawn in a worried frown.

She had been President Larsen's secretary for a long time now. It was eleven years ago that she had been hired on a temporary basis when Mrs. Allee, President Magruder's secretary, had moved to California. And then a good many things had happened with rapidity—Dr. Magruder had died, an interim president had served for six months, and then a small spare man with thinning sandy hair and an infectious smile had accepted the presidency. And she had worked for him ever since, admiring him and sharing with him his successes and his rare, very rare, failures. She had helped Mrs. Larsen plan faculty teas. She had handled correspondence arranging camp sessions, trips, dental appointments, dance recitals, and hockey matches for the Larsen children, Kristin and Eric. She had worked for all of them, loved them all, and always been supremely confident that President Larsen would prevail in all situations.

For the first time in all those years, she was frightened. This was beyond his control. This could destroy him.

She looked across the desk at him. A decade changes a man. His thinning sandy hair had dwindled to graying tufts. His once plump, sun-reddened face had thinned and paled. Lines crinkled out from the corners of his eyes and a fine network of lines crisscrossed around his mouth.

He looked every one of his sixty years that morning. He sat behind his desk, absorbed in his thoughts. Then he nodded once sharply to himself and looked up at her.

"Annabelle, we have a good deal to arrange before the deans and vice-presidents arrive at ten." He glanced at his desk clock. Twenty-seven minutes. "First," he began briskly, "I want every department head notified that classes will be dismissed this afternoon and that faculty attendance at the rally is encouraged." He picked up his pipe and clenched it in his mouth. "But not Dean Gorman." He looked at her. "Make sure I have a chance to speak to the dean privately before the meeting gets underway at ten."

"Yes, sir," and she tried to answer as if it were any day, his instructions commonplace, but she couldn't keep the worry out of her voice.

He looked at her and smiled. "Don't be upset, Annabelle. We'll do our best. And that's all that mortal man can manage. Let's not shoulder the burdens of the gods."

And so he set to work, a calm and reasonable man.

"Get me Eben Petrowski on the phone, Annabelle. And put in a call for Jim Croydon, the chief engineer, and for the president of the men's pep club. I think his name is Allenby." He paused and made several cryptic notations on his legal pad: 2 x 12s ??, folding chairs from Fine Arts, maybe park dept., PA system. Then he dropped down the page and wrote Presentation to Deans.

He thought for a moment, started to write, then looked up and said, "Annabelle, when they begin to arrive, make sure that Dean Abernathy and Vice-President Walters don't sit next to each other." He checked over his list. "You can get started on those items. And use your own judgment on what calls to let through."

After she had left, he began to outline what he would shortly be saying to his deans and vice-presidents. He was nearing the bottom of the page when his telephone buzzed, signaling an incoming call.

He stared at the phone for a moment. Annabelle wouldn't let any call through unless she considered it imperative. Slowly he lifted the receiver.

"President Larsen," Annabelle said nervously, "I have Governor Macklin on line three."

"Very good," he said quietly, but he knew that it wasn't good at all.

The line clicked open and a deep mellow voice said, "President Larsen? This is Governor Macklin."

"It's good of you to call, Governor."

"Of course, of course. I want to work with you in this difficult situation." He paused. "My office has been besieged with calls."

"Yes," President Larsen responded noncommittally.

"In fact, President Larsen, I have also received a call from Major General Wellington. You know the general, of course."

President Larsen did know the general, the reserve officer who commanded the National Guard. In Larsen's view, Wellington was first-rate at stocks and bonds (a senior vice-president with Botts and Kanaly Brokerage House), but intolerant to any whose views differed from his own.

But he replied mildly, "Yes, I know the general."

"Well, the general's son, Tom, is in the ROTC down there and . . ."

Oh God, Larsen thought.

". . . and Tom called his father and said there was absolutely no excuse for those long-haired types. He said those hippies wouldn't let the cadets drill. And he told his father there are a lot of rumors down there that there's going to be big trouble this afternoon at that so-called memorial rally. Memorial rally! So I've called to offer you the support of the National Guard. In fact, the general said he would be delighted to bring his men down there to help out."

President Larsen felt sure the general would indeed be delighted.

"I'm grateful, Governor, for the support shown by you and General Wellington. However, we aren't in an armed state of insurrection. The confrontation yesterday was an isolated incident, not at all typical of past protests. I think it all resulted from poor judgment shown by a good many who were involved and . . ."

Governor Macklin interrupted sharply. "Not on the part of the ROTC cadets, as I understand the situation."

President Larsen continued smoothly, "Certainly not on the part of the cadets. The cadet commander did the best he could in a very difficult situation. There has been no criticism of the cadets. You may reassure the general on that point. But as I was saying, Governor, the outlook for this afternoon is very, very good. We expect a calm assembly of students and faculty . . ."

"Aren't you pandering to these longhairs?" the governor demanded.

"No," President Larsen replied quietly. "I hope you will understand, Governor, that opposition to the ROTC is quite strong among the general run of students. This is not a 'hippie' or 'new left' movement. This protest is very general. This afternoon's rally will bring out very typical students, not political activists."

"Then why are there all these rumors saying there will be twice as big a riot as the one yesterday?"

"Because there are those who would like to see that happen. But we don't intend to let it happen."

"If the Guard is there, it can't happen," the governor said heavily.

President Larsen paused, then he said firmly, "I made it quite clear to newsmen only a little while ago, Governor, that I would call the National Guard to the campus only if we became involved in a true guerrilla action."

The governor made no response for a long moment. Then he, too, said very firmly, "I will be making an announcement to the press shortly, President Larsen, to report that I offered to call out the National Guard and that you refused to permit them on the campus." He paused again, then concluded, "I feel I can do no less to show to the people of our great state that I am concerned about the welfare of their children at the university."

President Larsen smiled a grim little smile. "I know the parents across the state will appreciate your concern, Governor. Please do be assured that the university will call for the Guard if it feels itself threatened with armed warfare."

"Very well, President Larsen," the governor said shortly. "I hope for your sake that you have done the right thing."

When the telephone line echoed emptily in his ear, President Larsen slowly put down the receiver. He remembered that he had warned the student editor to be sure and not ever fall down. It was good advice then. It was good advice now.

He stared down at his gleaming desk top, then realized suddenly that he was looking at his shadow. He swung around and looked out the tall broad window. Yes, the sun was shining.

A weak, watery sun, but sun nevertheless. So not even the weather was going to be an ally today. He had half-counted on the cold wet rain to discourage a large turnout. Now he must bend every effort to forestalling trouble.

Briskly he picked up the receiver and began to dial. There was so little time and so much to be done.

13

ROOM FOR CHARLEY

The red-and-white painted stripes on the long barricade glistened in the pale, watery sunlight.

Martin Henley jammed on the brakes of the little Renault and it bucked to a stop, its nose right up to the barricade that blocked off Hurlburt where it ran past the Greenway.

Martin stared and didn't want to believe what he saw.

A campus policeman in a bright orange slicker motioned him to back up and turn left onto Frost. When he made no move, the policeman frowned and began to walk toward the car.

"This whole area is blocked off today to make it easier for people to walk to the rally that's scheduled here this afternoon."

Martin's mouth thinned. So that was the story for the cops to tell all the suckers. Yeah. It made it easy for pedestrians—and threw a nice neat zone of control around the entire Greenway. Then Martin looked beyond the barricades at the workmen busy on the Greenway and for an instant felt something akin to panic. A work crew was busy unloading stacks of folding chairs from pickup trucks. Other workmen were setting the chairs in place in long rows that curved in semicircles around the half-finished speakers' stand.

"You'll have to back up and go left on Frost," the slicker-clad policeman directed.

Martin nodded. He took one more long look at the scurrying workmen on the Greenway, then slammed the Renault into reverse, lunged the little car backward, shoved the gear into first, and squealed off to the left on Frost.

The cop raised his hand angrily, then as the little car barreled down the street, shrugged and turned back toward the barricades.

Martin controlled his anger and eased up on his speed. He didn't have time to be angry. He had underestimated Larsen and he had to come up with something quick or this afternoon would be a complete bust.

He looked down at his watch. Almost eleven. He should have checked the Greenway earlier! But there had been so much to do: leaflets to stack for passing out at the rally, kids to be instructed on how to move a crowd forward and how to get a good chant going.

He stopped at the street light at Frost and Evans, his face drawn in a tight frown. Larsen had out-thought him all the way along the line. The first shock had been the TV announcement that classes were dismissed to encourage attendance at the rally. That would put the kids in a good mood. Martin didn't want anybody in a good mood. The second shock was the cordoned-off Greenway, the almost completed speakers' stand, and the long curving rows of chairs. His group wouldn't be able to move the crowd forward if it were seated!

But most of all, he felt cheated that President Larsen hadn't called out the National Guard. If the Guard had been called up,

Martin felt sure he could stage a true revolt. But Larsen had made it clearer than clear that he wasn't having the Guard at any price. So there was no point in hoping.

Martin gnawed on his lower lip. What could he possibly do to gain control?

The signal light flashed green. The car behind him honked impatiently. Martin looked up, shifted to first, and the Renault jumped ahead. About mid-way up the block, Martin turned abruptly into a parking lot.

He pulled into an empty slot, turned off the motor, and reviewed what he had done so far. He had concentrated on spreading word over the campus about Billy Kessler. He and Kathryn, hoarse from hours on the telephone, had milked every possible drop of outrage from their listeners. He had planned to use Billy's name to move the crowd forward, perhaps in a march on the armory. But President Larsen, with his seated audience and speakers' stand, would have the action under control.

Speakers' stand.

Martin kneaded his right cheekbone with his knuckles.

Speakers' stand.

Martin's eyes narrowed in thought. Maybe. Just maybe. He started the Renault, eased out of the parking slot, and turned west again on Frost. He drove slowly, watching for the big blue bell that would signal a telephone booth.

And when he was dialing, he was trying to figure a plausible approach.

"H'lo," an unfamiliar voice answered.

"Charley Sinclair there?" Martin asked.

"No."

"Happen to know where he is?"

"You might try the Student Senate office."

"Thanks."

Martin hung up and wiped his face with the back of his hand. Sure, that's where Charley would be today, trying to figure out what advantage he could wring from the rally. Martin nodded. He wouldn't call. It would be better to go over there. Much better.

Charley Sinclair lounged back in the swivel chair behind his desk, six feet two inches of relaxed satisfaction. He was the center of an admiring circle, but he was being graceful about it. He waved a big hand in self-deprecation. "It wasn't anything really," he said modestly. "I mean, what's one resolution more or less."

Al Forster, a political science major grateful for inclusion in Charley's group, made the expected response. "It wasn't just a resolution," he cried. "Charley, you captured the mood of the university. Why, it's your resolution that will bring everyone to the rally today! Everybody's talking about it."

And the others nodded and said, "That's right," and "That's what I think," and "Charley deserves the credit."

Charley shrugged, then admitted, "Sometimes I think I do have a feel for this sort of thing." And he looked around his office at his friends and he was tremendously content.

Charley Sinclair did try not to be a proud person. He remembered his mother's warning, "Now you don't be too full of yourself, Charles Sinclair. That'll get you in trouble." But it was difficult because, of his many qualities, he lacked humor. And without humor it is hard to maintain perspective, especially if you are six foot two and blond and handsome and able and, for the moment, triumphant. Delightfully, magnificently triumphant.

He greeted Martin Henley with a warm smile. "Martin. Good to see you this morning. What can I do for you?" Charley might have been running for the United States Senate.

Martin smiled diffidently. "Nothing, Charley. I just dropped by because I wondered what you were going to put in your speech."

"My speech," Charley repeated blankly.

Martin nodded. "Yeah. I saw the speakers' stand they're putting up on the Greenway and I figured that you'd be speaking. Especially since you were the author of the Student Senate resolution approving the rally."

Charley was proud and humorless and not past taking credit for an idea that wasn't his, but he wasn't an out-and-out phony. He frowned and the satisfied happiness seeped out of his face.

"I don't know anything about the speakers' stand," he said slowly. Then he added stiffly, "And nobody's asked me to speak."

"That's strange," Martin said, his voice puzzled. "The whole point of the rally is to provide a forum for students and that means student leaders, of course." Martin paused, then his frown faded. "I'll bet they've been trying to call you at your dorm. Because surely they'd plan to have the president of the Student Senate on the platform!"

"I know what," Al said eagerly, "I'll call President Larsen's office and ask."

Charley thought about it for a moment, then slowly nodded.

"I suppose that would be the right thing to do—for the sake of the Senate, of course."

So Al made the call and Charley and Martin, for very dissimilar reasons, waited tensely to hear the outcome.

Miss Scott answered and Al said very importantly, "This is Al Forster, calling from the office of the president of the Student Senate." He paused to let the full import of this reach Miss Scott, then he continued briskly, "We wanted to check and see if there had been some kind of oversight. That is, we wanted to know if there was a place on the speakers' stand for the Student Senate president, Charles Sinclair."

He listened, then said, "Sure." Cupping his hand over the receiver, he said softly, "She's going to check. She said she didn't know who was supposed to be on the platform."

Charley still leaned back in his chair, but the muscles ridged in his neck and his body felt heavy. Martin hunched close to the desk, scarcely breathing.

In the president's office, Miss Scott flicked on the intercom. "Dr. Larsen?" And there was a hint of laughter in her voice.

"Yes, Annabelle."

"I have a query on the phone from the Student Senate. They want a place on the speakers' stand for their president."

"My, oh my, there's just nothing like a speakers' stand, is there, Annabelle?" he said lightly. "Sure, sure, tell them he can come and welcome." Then his voice sobered. "Now I'd better get back to the meeting. I believe we're about to conclude."

Miss Scott flicked off the intercom and returned to line two and Al Forster. "President Larsen says that your president is welcome on the platform."

Al thanked her and put down the phone and said casually, "Sure, Charley, they're expecting you on the speakers' stand."

Charley Sinclair quickly sat up straight and reached for a notepad. He had been a national debate champion twice and he knew that preparation is much more than half the battle. Already he could see it in his mind, the crowd of students spread across the Greenway, the university officials on the platform, the television cameras—and Charley Sinclair.

Martin came around behind the desk. "About your speech . . ."

14

BILLY

The winter sunlight, its warmth magnified by the window glass, spread over Billy's bed, laving him with soft heat. He turned the palm of his left hand up to the warmth and for the first time in so long he was aware of something beyond the pain.

He looked too big for the narrow hospital bed even though he lay rigid. Every muscle in his body was tensed against the pain.

His head throbbed with a deep pervading ceaseless anguish. A river of pain burned from his empty eye socket down his face and deep into his neck and arm. The cast on his right arm added to his misery, its weight seeming to pull him down into the bed.

He licked at his dry cracked lips.

"Billy? Billy? Are you awake?"

Annette. He thought her name and wondered if he had imagined the words and then they came again as soft and gentle as the sweep of a bird's wing.

"Billy? Oh Billy."

And at the grief and love in her voice, he opened his eye and he saw her sitting in the bright sunlight whose warmth had helped pull him up out of unconsciousness. She saw the flicker of his eye toward the window and she rose and reached out for the Venetian blind cord.

"No, don't shut it."

The words came out in a hoarse whisper and he realized how terribly thirsty he was. He wanted water but the violence of the pain was too great to try and speak again.

He heard the sharp clink of a glass and the rushing crackle of water being poured over ice. He wanted the water so badly but he knew he couldn't lift his head. The pain would destroy him.

He felt the coolness of a plastic straw, gentle against his lips, and then, sweet and cold, the water came. He drank and drank and drank until Annette said softly, "Billy, maybe you'd better not drink any more for a while." Reluctantly he let loose the straw.

The water and the warmth of the sun together formed a bright edge outside the black core of his pain.

He felt Annette's light touch on his uninjured shoulder. "The nurse left some pills for the pain. She said you would need them." She paused. "Honey, can you hear me? The pills will help. Oh, Billy, I know it hurts so much." And her voice shook.

Something to help the pain. Something to give him ease. He was readying himself to make the effort to speak when the telephone on the night stand buzzed.

Annette stared at it for a moment, but when it rang again she yanked up the receiver.

"Hello." Her small heart-shaped face was pale with fatigue. Dark shadows spread under her eyes. And there was an unaccustomed look of wariness, an air of dogged defiance against all comers. She expected danger from all sources now. She was protecting her own as best she could.

She listened and began to frown, and then for a moment a corrosive anger twisted her delicate features. “Of course he can’t talk to you! Do you know what’s been done to him? He’s in pain, terrible pain, and you want to ask him questions! Well, he can’t talk to anybody.”

A voice crackled on the wire.

She said quickly, “No, he doesn’t know anything about it, anything at all! He’s been unconscious since last night. He’s very sick. Now leave us alone!” And she slammed down the receiver.

“Annette.” He spoke very quietly because it hurt to move his face at all.

She leaned close to him and touched his left hand. “You don’t have to worry about anything right now,” she said stubbornly, and she reached for the small white paper cup on the night stand. She picked it up and rolled the two oblong yellow pills into her hand.

“Annette.”

She would have resisted answering but she knew her Billy. If he was determined then he would know. And the more he had to ask, the more pain he would bear. She couldn’t stand to see him suffer, to see him form her name so carefully because the facial muscles that moved when he spoke pulled on the tissue underneath that empty socket.

She spoke quickly to forestall that carefully-mouthed demand. “It was Jake Stuart. He wanted to know if you supported the move to get Dean Gorman fired.”

He tried to think. It was very hard to think, to focus his mind on this demand. Why should Jake call wanting to know this of him? Why should Jake think he would support such a move?

He looked at Annette and he felt sure that something important was happening that he did not know about.

“Annette.” And his voice was stern.

She stared back at him and slowly her shoulders sagged in defeat.

"You can't do anything about it," she cried. "You can't!"

But she read the command in his eye and she told him. "There's to be another rally on the Greenway. Today. And the kids are saying Gorman ought to be fired."

He knew her so well and he knew with a calm certainty that there was more, that she was not telling him all of it.

He began to struggle to pull himself up and she cried, "Stop. Stop!" And then she said, "All right, Billy. When I went out for breakfast this morning, I found a leaflet." She reached across and picked up her purse from the window sill. "They're all over the campus." She pulled a crumpled pale blue sheet out of her purse and read it to him, her voice flat and empty.

BOOT ROTC!
CAN GORMAN!
OR STRIKE!
REMEMBER WHAT THEY DID TO BILLY KESSLER!
COME TO THE GREENWAY 2 P.M. THURSDAY
LET'S TELL THEM SO THEY HEAR. YOU KNOW WHAT THEY DID.
YOU KNOW WHO DID IT. DON'T LET THEM THINK THEY'RE
GETTING AWAY WITH IT.
BOOT ROTC!
CAN GORMAN!
OR STRIKE!

She met his gaze now and began to fight what she saw in that one clear vivid eye. "Billy, I heard on the news this morning, President Larsen said he won't fire the dean. So it will be all right. He won't fire the dean and . . ."

Her voice faded as she thought through what she had said.

Then she rushed on, "Just because this stupid leaflet calls for a strike doesn't mean it will happen! It's only a threat."

Billy sagged back on the hard pillow. Sweat beaded his face, dampening his beard. His good eye glazed over and he fought against the pain that seemed to be expanding and worsening, the deep bone-wrenching ache of the empty socket, the steady drumming throb of the outraged nerves, the pinched anguish of the multilated skin. He lay there and fought the pain that was trying to sweep him down the dark river into oblivion.

Dimly he heard the door open and the soft murmur of voices. Questioningly, he called out, "Suzie?"

She heard the hoarse, strained whisper and came across the room to murmur softly, "Billy, I didn't mean to wake you." Her gaze flinched away from the bandage-swathed head but she reached down to hold his left hand. "How are you feeling?"

He frowned, not really hearing her, his mind trying to force itself beyond the pain to confront a dimly-perceived responsibility.

"Suzie."

She bent closer to him and smelled the sweet, clinging odor of anesthetic and blood and sweat. "Rest now, Billy. Annette and I will take care of everything."

"The leaflets!" he said sharply, impatiently. "Have you seen the leaflets?"

She drew a quick breath. "Yes," she said reluctantly. How could Annette have been fool enough to let him know about the leaflets?

As if in answer to her unspoken rebuke, perhaps in actual response to her quick questioning glance, Annette said bitterly, "Jake Stuart called. He wanted to know if Billy wanted Dean Gorman fired."

Suzie closed her eyes briefly. How could Jake have done

that? Jake knew how badly Billy was hurt. How could Jake have done it?

Billy was trying to rise up. Suzie leaned closer and held tightly to his hand and said quickly, "Lie still, Billy. I saw the leaflets, yes, but they won't succeed. President Larsen won't fire the dean. I heard it on the news."

Billy nodded almost imperceptibly. His voice was so dry and scratchy, she had to listen closely to understand him. "They know he won't fire the dean. That's why they asked for it."

"But that doesn't make any sense," Suzie objected.

"Oh yeah," he said softly. "They pick a symbol, somebody like me, and play it so big that I'm hurt. Then comes the huge demand, kick out ROTC, fire the dean." He paused, then forced himself on. "They know Larsen won't do it. Then they'll call for a strike."

Annette was by the bed now, too. And her thin voice demanded desperately, "OK. If the dean doesn't get fired, then let them strike! Why should we care?"

"Because they're using my name to cause a strike. And because a university is a place where everybody should be able to speak. A strike'll shut it down. And kids with nothing to do—there'll be trouble."

He took a deep breath, then demanded, "What time is it?"

Suzie glanced down at her watch. "It's almost one-thirty."

"What time does the rally start?"

She hesitated, then said slowly, "Two o'clock."

He lifted his big bandaged head, then with agonizing slowness managed to hoist himself up on his left elbow.

"Annette, please."

She and Suzie both helped him to sit up all the way. He gripped his wife's arm so hard that she had to bite her lip not to cry out. He waited for a long moment until the pain in his head seemed to recede a little.

"Those pills," he said grimly.

He swallowed them down and drank the fresh cold water and sat unmoving on the edge of the bed. Finally, gradually, the pain ebbed a little. But he knew he couldn't gather strength much longer.

"Annette. Your transistor. Get it."

She reached for her purse and pulled out the small, oblong radio and flicked it on. Static crackled. She fiddled with the dial and, abruptly, the newscaster's voice filled the room.

". . . an undercurrent of grim determination pervades the university campus as students marshal on the Greenway to protest the violence that marred an anti-ROTC rally here yesterday. The stage is set for an angry confrontation, the students demanding the ouster of Dean of Students Robert Gorman in reparation for the maiming of student leader Billy Kessler, and university President Kenneth Larsen remaining adamant in his refusal to fire the dean. The impasse may well result in a strike that will close down the state's largest university. We will switch now to the KBS correspondent at the State Capitol, Bruce Benton, who will bring us up to date on Governor Macklin's response to this latest crisis in . . ."

15

A GRAVE CHARGE

Kathryn slipped through the crowd. She had worked to the very last minute, passing out leaflets in the Union, urging students to come. Her eyes glittered with excitement and she broke into a half-run. And then, when she pushed past a thick knot of kids and saw the Greenway spreading out before her, she stopped so abruptly that someone behind bumped into her. She stood there and stared, stricken.

She looked at the speakers' stand, complete with two lines of folding chairs and a lectern and cables draped over the side for a PA system. She stared at the long curving lines of chairs set up on the Greenway. Most were filled now. And scattered all across the Greenway were members of the University Pep Club, conspicuous in their brilliant yellow shirts, serving as ushers.

People pushed past her and still she stood, sick with dismay. And then she saw Martin standing tensely near the speakers' stand. She slipped and squirmed and pushed her way up to him and clutched his arm.

"They've made fools of us!" she hissed.

He ignored her and continued to search among the dignitaries seated on the platform. Then, abruptly, his tension slacked. His forward-thrust face, beaked and predatory, remained palely expressionless but the sense of urgency had gone.

Kathryn felt the easing of the muscles in his arm and that goaded her to fresh fury. She looked up and down the Greenway and saw nothing good.

The thin sunlight couldn't warm the arctic air mass that had pushed down into the state over the night but the clouds that had stretched like gray wool earlier in the morning were gone, swept away by the shift of the wind to the south. And,with the cloud cover gone, the pale sunlight cheered even if it didn't warm. So, again, they had come by the hundreds to the Greenway, students of all shapes and sizes and sorts and faculty members ranging from the mod to the musty. They came very quietly and took their seats.

This orderly, mannerly massing of people meant the failure of everything Martin had planned. Everything, really, that he had promised her! Her fingers tightened painfully on his arm. "It looks like a Parks Department spectacular, seats for everybody and everybody welcome! The next thing you know, there'll be a sorority skit up on the platform." She looked him up and down disdainfully. "You poor fool. President Larsen must be laughing at you!"

"Shut up."

"I won't shut up!" she retorted and her voice rose. "This is a fiasco, a complete . . ." Even Kathryn quailed at the look in his ice blue eyes.

"There are some things you don't know, Kathryn. Now, be quiet."

She was quiet and docile enough to follow him to seats

mid-way down the Greenway. But everything she saw spelled disaster to their hopes. There was no way Martin could pull it off.

She was not alone in her conviction that the rally was going to be peaceful. Chief Eben Petrowski stood on the highest point of the bluff that marked the western edge of the Greenway, watching the orderly scene below. Everything he saw reinforced his belief that they had it knocked. By God, Larsen was a genius! The grassy plain had been transformed into the equivalent of an outdoor meeting hall with everyone in his appointed place and the whole area neatly cordoned off!

He watched the entire scene for a moment longer, then lifted his powerful field glasses and slowly began to quarter the area, looking for anything off-key, anything that might hint of potential danger. At length, he lowered the glasses, confident that everything was under control.

Jake Stuart stood near the speakers' stand, surveying the Greenway with a jaundiced expression. He, too, felt sure it was all under the control of the university and he wondered at the stupidity of his fellow students that they apparently didn't see how they were being manipulated. He watched, his blocky head thrust forward, and decided the next thing would probably be an award of Administrator of the Year to Dean Gorman.

One of the ubiquitous yellow-shirted Pep Club members bounded up to him. "There are some seats toward the back." When Jake ignored him, the young man said good-naturedly, "Hey, buddy, would you mind moving on? We're trying to keep this lane up to the speakers' stand open."

Jake looked at him briefly. "Press."

"OK," the young man responded. "There's a special section for the press." He took Jake by the arm. "See?" And he pointed to a double row of ten chairs set at a right angle to the platform, affording an excellent view of both the stand and the audience.

Jake stood bullishly for a moment more, then nodded at the usher and ambled toward the reserved section. He might as well watch the show in comfort. He settled in a front-row seat, nodded to Ryan of AP, then flipped open his notebook and began to sketch a tentative lead:

It's a mechanical world. Push a button and a doorbell rings. Flip a switch and the light comes on. On the Greenway Thursday, President Larsen had them set up some chairs—and the students came and sat down. A mechanical thing—somebody provides you with a seat and that's where you put your rear. But they were more than seats on the . . .

The loudspeaker crackled. Responding to the familiar stimulus, most students looked toward the speakers' stand and the rumble of conversations fell away.

Oh, you robots, Jake thought. You perforated, punched, programmed, Pavlovian automatons. Sit straight. Clap pretty. Hand it to him on a silver salver.

President Larsen stood behind the lectern. His measured gaze swept the Greenway. He waited with the instinct of the accomplished lecturer for the right moment to begin. He would have been surprised to know that Eben Petrowski and Jake Stuart already accounted the afternoon his, awarding him the game though the hands had yet to be played. Had he known, he would have shaken his head gently and perhaps reminded them of Aesop's warning not to count upon unhatched chickens. As it was, he did not know of their certainty. He looked out over the Greenway and felt instead a great awareness of the fluidity and fragility of the moment.

As he waited for silence to fall, the moment seemed as

insubstantial as a dream. Now everything was peace and order. What would it be when the afternoon ended?

When it was still, he began quietly.

"Ladies and gentlemen, it is good of all of you to come here this cold and damp afternoon. We are here to mark an important moment in the life of the university."

He looked thoughtfully out across the Greenway at the hundreds of intent young faces.

"There is a grave charge abroad. There are those who say that the violence here yesterday was a deliberate planned assault by the university administration against student dissidents."

They listened, watchful, wary, hostile,

Into the taut silence, he declared, "This charge is false."

He gripped the sides of the lectern. "You may fairly ask how you are to know which is true. Sophocles told us that 'truth ever has most strength of what men say' and I think he is right. I believe that the truth has a ring like crystal. I believe that if we study what happened on the Greenway we can decide as reasoning men what seems credible as its cause."

Calmly, honestly, he recalled the gathering of the students and the arrival of the cadets, the maneuvering for control of the Greenway, Chief Petrowski's attempts to separate cadets and protesters, Dean Gorman's arrival, his command that the Greenway be cleared, the moving line of policemen, the wounding of Captain Bristow, the attack.

"This is what happened. Now let us consider these questions. Is it credible that the university planned this confrontation?" Slowly, he shook his head. "In point of fact, Dean Gorman was called to the scene at a late moment by a member of the ROTC staff. Even if you feel that the dean lacked the authority or the moral right to order students from university property, you cannot fairly assume that he intended for the police to attack the students."

President Larsen emphasized that the attack was in response to the wounding of Captain Bristow.

He paused and searched the faces of the students in the first row and he saw a grudging response, a beginning acceptance.

A girl sitting behind Kathryn said, "I think he's right! It's silly to think the university planned a riot!"

Kathryn twisted in her seat. "Silly? What's silly is how pitifully easy it is to fool people like you! Who told the cops to get Billy Kessler? Tell me that!"

But Kathryn's heart was scarcely in it. The girl shrugged and ignored her and all across the Greenway kids were nodding in acceptance.

Jake Stuart watched and his face was sardonic. Larsen didn't know it, but he wasn't home free yet. The *Gazette* editorial would pose a few of the more awkward questions tomorrow. Like, how about ROTC? And if Gorman hadn't brought the cops, there couldn't have been any violence, so how about that, coach?

On the speakers' stand, President Larsen gave them time. "I would like to conclude by responding to the specific demands made by some students. I will say very strongly that I do not think a man should be dismissed because he makes a mistake. There are students across the campus and graduates across this nation who remember Dean Gorman with warmth and gratitude because he bent every effort to helping them secure scholarships and part-time jobs so that they might stay in school. One afternoon cannot wipe out the devoted work of years."

He stood, a small spare man, and looked forthrightly out from the platform. "And, finally, I would like to propose a dialogue with some student representatives concerning the continuance of ROTC on our campus. Perhaps a panel of students might debate me. I would hope to emphasize my view that the right of some students to enroll in the ROTC is as important to them as the right of other students to oppose the ROTC. I would suggest also that the United States Army is not a monolithic, evil body intent upon corrupting its soldiers but is a huge organization upon which the temporary civilian-bound officers have a tremendous and important effect. I believe that it would be foolish and perhaps dangerous to have all officers drawn from service academies."

He looked down at his audience and smiled. "But these are points for discussion. And, who knows? Perhaps your representatives might persuade me to change these views. I agree wholly with Marcus Aurelius, who said, 'If any man can convince me and bring home to me that I do not think or act aright, gladly will I change; for I search after truth, by which man never yet was harmed.'"

16

A GOLDEN VOICE

In the boxlike room on the third floor of St. Catherine's, Annette listened to the solid measured applause and looked up happily. "Billy, do you hear? Everything's going to be all right."

She finished lacing his right boot, then stood and picked up the transistor radio and turned it off.

"Turn it back on," he ordered.

"But, Billy," she cried, "it's all over and you need to rest."

"Turn it on."

She shrugged and twisted the knob and the full round tones of the announcer flowed into the room.

". . . is walking back to his seat on the speakers' stand. He has stopped to confer with someone. No list of speakers has been made available, but . . ."

His voice rolled on and on, slick, light, empty.

Annette smiled, her eyes glistening with relief. She smiled happily at Billy. "You won't have to go, Billy. I'll help you get these clothes off. I'm so glad, so glad. You shouldn't even be sitting up, much less trying to go to the campus!"

Billy didn't say anything. He sat awkwardly on the side of the bed, his left arm gouged straight into the hard mattress. His shirt bunched over his cast-laden right arm. It was only the strength of his left arm and grim determination that kept him upright.

Annette had her left arm around his back now to help him ease back down on the pillow.

He resisted her gentle pull.

"Billy, you heard the radio! It's all right now. You can rest."

He stared at her. The room wavered. He couldn't see Annette very clearly. Light and shadow blurred. He wanted so badly to lie down, to sink into drugged oblivion, free from pain and effort, free. But he couldn't. And he only dimly understood why. He hadn't intended to be a hero on the Greenway. He hadn't intended that at all. He only thought that if he spoke up and reached out a friendly hand he could stop that relentless march. He wasn't trying to be brave because he hadn't felt that there was anything to fear.

But because somebody had thrown a bottle and he had fallen under the police clubs, his name was being used to foment trouble.

He still had no desire to look or act like a hero, but only he could put a stop to this phony martyr business. Only he. So he sat on the edge of a hospital bed, big and hurt and sick at his stomach, his head a pulsating mass of pain, and held fast to his determination not to be exploited.

He would listen to the announcer. Maybe the people who'd printed those leaflets would give up, discouraged by President Larsen's speech. Maybe everything would turn out all right.

He listened. It began as meaningless shouts ridden under by the continuing patter of the announcer. Then the shouts picked up force and became distinct and Billy felt a curious wrenching inside himself as he understood them.

"Billy Kessler. Billy Kessler. Billy Kessler. Billy . . ."

He stared at the black plastic radio and listened to his name, loud and louder, booming, calling. He listened and anger stirred in his mind—and the curling edge of fear.

Annette's face flattened. She hated them, all of them. They didn't care about Billy. They were using his name in anger and hatred. It was an abomination to use his name like that!

She twisted the dial and the room was suddenly full of silence.

Billy didn't say anything, but he reached out and gripped the edge of the night stand and gradually eased off the bed to stand. He swayed on his feet, but Annette was there and holding him up and crying, "Billy, you can't go! You can't!"

He leaned against her, his left arm heavy around her shoulders. "I can do what I have to do . . . if you'll help me." And the last was added in a desperate whisper.

Tears slipped down her face. He knew she would always do whatever he asked.

Abruptly, the door to the room began to swing in. Both Billy and Annette were startled, but it wasn't a nurse or a sister.

Suzie was backing into the room, pulling inside an empty wheelchair and talking all the while. "Well, I got one! I don't know how soon it will be missed. It was parked outside a door marked Radiology so I just swiped it. I found the freight elevator. It's down the east hall and no one will see us from the desk, but I still . . ." She had turned around now and saw their faces. "What's happened now?"

Annette didn't answer. She drew a quivering breath and turned the radio on again.

". . . ler, Billy Kessler, Billy Kessler, Billy . . ."

Suzie gripped the frame of the wheelchair. "What does it mean?"

"I think . . ." Billy began and then a fresh clear voice sounded over the chant on the radio, a resonant virile magnetic voice, a golden voice.

"Please. Please. May I speak?"

And the three of them standing in the small hospital room could imagine the upraised arms, the opened hands. It was that kind of voice. They stared at the radio and waited.

The roar, the pulsing repetition of Billy's name waned. As it gradually grew quieter, the announcer said excitedly, "This impromptu show of concern for injured student leader Billy Kessler caused a huddle on the speakers' stand and, just a moment ago, Student Senate President Charles Sinclair apparently volunteered to speak to the students, many of whom are now standing, their right arms raised in the clenched fist salute. No one knows exactly what has been meant by the chant but it is conjectured—" The announcer broke off, then spoke rapidly. "Yes, yes, Sinclair is going to speak. Yes, here he is now . . ." And the announcer gave way to the clear golden tones of Charley Sinclair.

"Billy Kessler can't be here today. We understand that he lies at St. Catherine's Hospital now in very serious condition." Charley paused. "I cannot presume to speak for Billy and all of the other students who were beaten yesterday. But I can speak for those of us who are here today! And I can ask that justice be done!"

"Right on!" a voice shouted.

Charley Sinclair leaned across the lectern and thundered, "Who ordered that the students be removed from the Greenway?"

He waited and someone in the audience yelled, "Dean

Gorman!" and then another voice and another called out the dean's name.

"Who told the cops to get the kids?"

The kids were ready this time. Voices shouted loud and strong, "Dean Gorman! Dean Gorman!"

"Who do we want fired?"

"Dean Gorman! Dean Gorman!"

No more words were necessary in the narrow hospital room. Suzie pushed the wheelchair next to Billy and she and Annette helped him sit down. They tucked a tan-and-white hospital blanket around his shoulders and another over his legs.

Annette grabbed her coat from the small closet and shrugged into it. She turned off Charley Sinclair in mid-sentence ("We won't be . . .") and dropped the transistor into her purse. Suzie zipped her raincoat, then eased open the door.

Billy's room was only two doors away from the east wing, but his doorway lay in full view of the semicircular desk in the center of the main hallway. A nurse sat behind the counter, her head bent to read a folder spread out before her.

Suzie started to raise her hand in the gesture *follow me* when the red light above the next room flashed on. Suzie pushed the door almost shut and whispered, "Wait. The nurse'll be coming down the hall."

In a moment they heard the soft, firm tread go past. Then Suzie said softly, "Let's go," and they were in the hall and on their way. When they reached the end of the main hall and turned up the east wing, they felt a little safer. The hall seemed very long. At the end they could see the dark-brown metal doors of the huge freight elevator.

Mid-way down the hall, a door opened. A nurse's aide, burdened with a heavy armload of clean sheets, stepped out of the linen closet. She stopped, counted the pile of sheets, nodded to herself, shut the door, and turned to walk up the hall toward them.

The three of them felt as stiff as marionettes as the woman drew nearer and nearer. But she passed them by with a polite, incurious smile, her thoughts absorbed in the number of beds to be made, the medication schedule, four alcohol rubs, the dinner trays, and the fact that she had to get off work in time so she could take Sonny to Cub Scouts.

The three sighed with relief, then behind them they heard quick, tapping footsteps and a starchy rustle. One of the sisters had turned into the hall!

Annette's hands tightened on the sides of the wheelchair and for one wild, disloyal moment she hoped the sister would call out, stop them, demand to know where that patient was being taken. Annette slowed down, her feet responding to that unspoken wish.

Suzie dropped behind Annette. "Hurry," the dark girl whispered. "I'll walk behind and shield you two."

"Hurry," Billy urged.

Annette hesitated for just a moment, then she gave in without a battle and the wheelchair picked up speed. But it was still with a sharp pang of disappointment that she heard the nurse's aide stop the sister.

"Sister! Sister, I don't know what to do! Mae isn't at work today and I have beds to make in 307 and 308 and 321 and it's time for the alcohol rubs but I still don't have the . . ."

The soft, worried voice ran on while the two girls and the boy in the wheelchair waited for the elevator to rise.

Sister Mary Seraphina did notice the trio at the end of the hall and she wondered briefly why they were using the freight elevator, but her mind only touched the thought then returned to the distraught aide. She listened to the catalog of difficulties, then said gently, "I'll be happy to do the alcohol rubs, Harriet, then we'll see where we are. Now, which patients . . ."

And the sister didn't even hear the grudging clang as the doors of the old elevator opened,then closed again.

It was chilly inside the huge old cage, the unpadded sides holding in the cold, and it smelled strongly of disinfectant. The elevator descended laboriously. When it jolted to a stop at the first floor, the ponderous doors began to open.

Suzie leaned forward and realized immediately that they couldn't bluff their way through there. This was the Emergency Ward! She jabbed the button for the basement. The big doors slowly shut and the elevator lumbered on down the shaft.

But when the doors drew apart, the three of them hesitated, daunted by the dank cold of the wide cement hallway that was lighted only sparsely by unshaded bulbs spaced far apart.

Suzie stared out at the bleak, tunnel-like hall and decided instinctively that she didn't like it at all.

Then a light flashed on the elevator panel and the big doors began to rumble shut. Someone on an upper floor had rung for it.

And they had to decide at once what to do.

Annette stared unmoving at the bright pinpoint of red light on the panel. Suzie reached out to push the OPEN DOOR button. The big doors paused, then heavily moved back.

"We have to get out," Suzie said quickly.

Annette hesitated, then pushed the wheelchair out into the cold hall.

Suzie felt a nightmarish sense of isolation as the dark brown metal doors closed for the last time and the cage rumbled up the shaft without them. She looked down at Billy and the pallor of his face shocked her. He slumped in the wheelchair, his good eye closed, and she wondered with a pang of fear if he were unconscious. And if he weren't, he soon might be if they kept hauling him around. What did she and Annette think they were doing? Billy should be in bed!

His eye opened and he looked up. She almost spoke her thoughts, but he looked at her with such determination that she knew it would be useless, would do nothing more than wring strength from him, strength he couldn't spare.

She looked down at the huge young man, who seemed curiously shrunken in the wheelchair, at his matted brown hair and beard, at his broad, kind mouth now thinned by pain, and said quickly, "Don't worry, Billy, we'll find a way out. We'll get you to the rally,"

She turned away to hurry up the hall in search of an exit.

17

"WE'VE BEEN BETRAYED!"

Charles leaned over the lectern and jabbed his right hand at the audience. Charles had spent a good deal of thought on gestures, how effective and helpful they could be. The danger, of course, was in distracting your listeners, but he was careful. The trick was to save gestures for the moments of most impact.

The wind whipped against his face and a thick strand of blond hair flopped down on his forehead. He tossed it back, but not all the way. He hunched over the lectern and intoned, "We will not be denied." He paused, then thundered, "Justice will not be denied!"

The kids went wild. They shouted and screamed and yelled.

Sweat streamed down Charley's face. Even in the cold southerly wind, he was hot. But he sweated with triumph, with a delicious tingling excitement. It was like jumping a horse or making love to a girl. If you did it right, just so, it was fantastic!

He pulled air deep into his lungs, then held up both hands. Sweet power, sweet glory. The silence fell. He savored it to its limits, then, before his power waned, he spoke. "Dean Gorman ordered the kids off their own land! Dean Gorman turned the police on the kids! Dean Gorman loosed blood and violence on the Greenway." He paused and then he shouted, "There is no place on this campus for Dean Gorman!"

Two blocks to the north of the speakers' stand, in a spacious office on the third floor of the Administration Building, Dean Gorman leaned back in his desk chair and stared with mounting fury at the six-inch screen of his Sony.

That no-good Sinclair! That ungrateful son of a bitch. It would be a cold day in hell before he got another dime of scholarship money! But even as he thought it, the dean knew he couldn't do it. He could imagine the bleeding-heart cry that would go up if Charley Sinclair lost his scholarship.

The dean pulled out a pack of Benson & Hedges and lit one. The smoke irritated but at the same time soothed the inflamed membranes at the back of his throat. He smoked and watched Charley Sinclair offer him up to the crowd—and listened with growing uneasiness to the ugly sound of the shouts.

Ugly. He stared at the standing, shouting kids. They were ugly and they were making the world ugly. He could not understand them. They liked to look dirty and grubby, and they didn't work. They weren't like the people he'd gone to school with. They were lazy, physically and mentally. They didn't believe in anything but feeling! All this nonsense about feeling. It didn't matter how you felt. What mattered was your duty, your job.

Dean Gorman watched the screen, repelled but fascinated. Charley Sinclair had raised both arms now and clenched his right fist. The deep-throated howl of his listeners made Gorman feel cold.

God, they hated him! And why? Because he'd told the police

to move them off the Greenway. But they shouldn't have been blocking the Greenway. They didn't have any right!

But they were going to close down the university if Larsen didn't fire him. And though there was no love lost between them, Larsen wouldn't fire him because that would not, in the president's view, be honorable. Even though things would get very tough for Larsen if the students struck.

The chant grew louder and louder and soon it was a scream, "Gorman, no, Gorman, no, Gorman, no . . ."

Ugly people do ugly things, Dean Gorman thought, and fear curled around his thoughts. What if they tried to set his house on fire? Or bombed it? And in that instant, he made up his mind. He was going to get the hell out. He could probably ride it through, keep the job, if there were any campus or any job left when the strike ended. But at what price? What if somebody went after his kids?

His face flattened when he thought of Laura. If he said he was through, she would laugh at first, then she would swear. She liked it here, her bridge club, her garden group, the sculpting classes, the innumerable goddam things that always kept her away from home. Maybe, if they moved on, the kids would have a half-time mother for at least a while.

He pulled open his right-hand desk drawer and took out the letter from the brand-new junior college in Kansas City. It was a working-class school. Most of the students lived at home and had part-time jobs. They were the kind of students he understood. Strivers. He opened the letter and read it again and slowly nodded. His eyes narrowed. Laura wouldn't like it. In the academic pecking order, it was from nowhere. But he didn't care. He spread out the college's shiny brochure and smiled. And for the first time in years felt a glimmer of excitement and happiness.

As he read over the catalog, he didn't even listen to the TV as Sinclair wrapped it up and tied the bow. ". . . and the cops beat the kids right down into the ground. They gouged out Billy Kessler's eye. Now, are we going to act like it was just one of those little mistakes that anybody could make? Are we going to let them lay it on us and lay it on us?"

And the "No!" came back from a thousand throats.

The roaring response sounded like the rumble of far-off drums as it reverberated over Suzie's car radio.

She pressed harder on the accelerator. How many more blocks to the campus now? Five? Six? She glanced sideways at Billy. He hulked like a misshapen statue. His head hung forward, his face was ashen and clammy. Had his arduous climb up the basement stairs and the stumbling, lumbering agony across the uneven, weed-clumped hospital lawn, had that weakened him so much that it didn't really matter how many blocks were left?

The pressure of her foot on the accelerator eased.

"Billy, are you all right? Billy?"

He didn't move. He didn't open his eye. His voice was so low she could barely hear, but he did answer. "Hurry, Suzie."

She hesitated, then pressed her right foot down and the car picked up speed, hurtling down the humpy asphalted street toward the campus. The speedometer needle crept past 50, edged toward 60. Then, gratefully, she remembered the dip in the pavement at Crown and Holley. She had to slow down. Billy couldn't fault her for slowing down for a dip. Even so, she hit it going 30 and the car whammed hard on the steep, sharp ascent.

Annette had seen the jolt coming and wrapped her arms around Billy. "Slow down, Suzie! Slow down!"

But the roar was louder on the radio and now through the open car window they could hear the shouts on the Greenway.

"Gorman must go! Gorman must go! Gorman must go!"

Then, sharply over the radio, crisply on the PA, sounded President Larsen's voice.

"Ladies and gentlemen. Ladies and gentlemen, please!"

The loud, hoarse chant continued.

"Ladies and gentlemen, you are shouting for me to fire Dean Gorman."

The shouting lessened a little. Some of them listened.

"Ladies and gentlemen, the meanest, most despicable of criminals in our society is by right due a trial by jury. We no longer live by the rule of the lynch mob. But this afternoon you are asking me to return to the lawlessness of sacrifice and appeasement. And I tell you that so long as I am president of this university, we will live by the rule of reason or we will not . . ."

And his voice, loud and firm as it was, could no longer be heard above the shouts of "Strike! Strike! Strike!"

Suzie's Mustang hurtled down the diagonal street of Wheeler and squealed left onto Hurlburt. The Greenway lay directly ahead now. Hundreds of kids stood, their right arms raised high in the clenched-fist salute. Those in front were beginning to spill out of the rows and into the aisles, moving toward the platform, and their cry was thunderous in the chill October air.

"Strike! Strike! Strike!"

A police whistle shrilled as the little red Mustang roared down Hurlburt. Suzie saw the red-and-white striped blockades. She hesitated, slowed the car, then veered to the right.

"Hang on!" she yelled.

The Mustang bumped up over the curb onto the Greenway.

The campus policeman on Hurlburt hesitated. His orders were to stay back of the Greenway unless specifically called closer. But what was that Mustang doing? He switched on his walkie-talkie. "Mustang evading barricade, entering Greenway. What instructions?"

Chief Petrowski, high on the bluff, had seen the barrel-house approach of the small red car, too. He had focused his powerful field glasses on the compact as it lurched up over the curbing. He saw the dark-haired girl driver, her face strained, intent. He saw the big awkwardly seated young man with the thick brown beard and bandaged head and next to him a small blond girl.

The car gained the thick, winter-pale grass and angled more to the south and he recognized Billy Kessler.

What to do about the car? He could have it stopped but he knew that the cost of stopping it would be greater than he was willing to bear.

"Let the red Mustang proceed," he said quietly. "Let the red Mustang proceed."

Then he lowered the walkie-talkie and watched the car's bumpy progress across the Greenway. It squeezed between two sycamores, rolled along the roped-off seats, and drew ever nearer to the platform.

The crowd was falling silent, startled by the roaring arrival of the Mustang. Everyone turned and stretched, trying to see what was happening. The shouting dwindled and a curious expectancy settled over the Greenway.

The car lurched to a stop by the east side of the speakers' stand.

Suzie jumped out and ran around to the opposite side as Annette stepped out and held open the door.

It took him a long moment to edge along the seat,then turn enough to put his legs out and try to stand. The girls both bent forward to help.

When he stood, hunched forward a little as if pulled by the weight of the cast on his right arm, and slowly turned to look out across the Greenway, the crowd was utterly silent. The only sound was of the wind, the creak of winter-bare branches, and the crackling rustle of tumbling leaves.

Then the big, leonine head bandaged, the hair and beard matted, turned slowly to study the platform.

The speakers' stand, a temporary structure of pine two-by-twelves, reared six feet above the ground. The only stairway had been built at the west end. No need for access at both ends in a structure to be torn down that evening.

So Billy looked at the platform and his good eye traveled its length to the steps at the far end and thirty feet had never looked so long before. Everyone looked with him and every heart ached at the distance.

President Larsen watched and knew that what happened from this moment forward was completely beyond his control. Whatever was the tune to which this young man marched would be the tune piped this day. For a man so committed to the rational but so resigned to the fates it was a pointed reminder of the limitations upon man's control of his destiny. President Larsen watched the young man move slowly, so slowly, with such evident effort in front of the platform, and knew the future of the university was in the lap of the gods.

Billy had no such thoughts. His only goal was somehow to reach those steps and somehow to climb them. He managed to keep going, a step at a time, Suzie on his right, Annette on his left. He moved as if each step were an enemy to master.

The kids waited with a rare patience and empathy.

Dean Hamilton of the College of Law hurried down the steps. A big man, too, he supported Billy effortlessly and the girls stood back. Up on the platform, President Larsen pulled a chair forward and helped Billy sit down. As he handed him the microphone, he said, "I admire your courage."

Billy held the microphone in his left hand and stared out across the Greenway. The wind fluttered the edges of the blanket that hung around his shoulders. Billy turned his face a little to the right so that the brunt of the chilly wind would strike the uninjured side of his face.

He sat, gathering strength. The kids waited and their anger was gone. Perhaps it was the very quietness of Billy's person that had calmed them.

When Billy spoke, his voice was low and thin. It lacked the full-bodied resonance of Charley's. It was merely a voice. But they listened.

"Please don't strike," he said simply. "Please don't."

He took a deep breath. "They've used my name to ask you to strike. They want you to strike if Dean Gorman isn't fired." He frowned and the words came very slowly. "I don't know how to explain it, but yesterday just happened. It wasn't anybody's fault."

A low rumble of surprise and disagreement stirred his listeners. He held up his hand and it was quiet again.

"But what happened yesterday isn't the important thing," he said. "What matters is peace. What matters is closing the campus to the ROTC. And a strike won't do that. It will only cause trouble."

He paused and sagged in his chair, and it was with a tremendous effort that he lifted his head again and pled, "Please don't strike. Don't listen to the ones who want to cause trouble. We want peace, not quarrels. Please."

And he had said all that he could say.

President Larsen walked quickly to him and took the microphone. "Ladies and gentlemen, you have had the rare privilege of hearing a courageous and disciplined man." The president paused, then asked, "Will you accept him as one of your spokesmen on the question of banning the ROTC? If you will, please say 'aye.'"

The ayes thundered.

President Larsen nodded. Then he smiled. "I've probably spun my own web but that's as may be. I will look forward to debating the issue of banning ROTC with Mr. Kessler here on the Greenway two weeks from today. That will give Mr. Kessler time to gain strength—and it will give me time to pray a lot. Thank you, ladies and gentlemen, for coming today. Godspeed until we meet again."

He turned away—and the confrontation was over.

Eben Petrowski felt as though he'd climbed a mountain and come back down again.

Jake Stuart was torn between anger and disgust.

But Kathryn Ellington felt defrauded and betrayed. She jumped to her feet and glared at those around her who were beginning to walk quietly away, talking in low and serious tones. She watched them go and then she shouted, "Strike! Strike!"

Martin grabbed her by the arm but she shook him off.

"Strike! Strike!" she screamed.

Those nearby looked at her, then quickly looked away. Some frowned. A few laughed. Tears of fury and frustration burned her eyes.

"You fools!" she cried. "You fools, we've been betrayed! Don't you see it? We've been betrayed!"

18

STEP BY STEP

Kathryn slammed the door to her apartment so hard that the flimsy wood of the frame shook. She flicked up the light switch, then stood just inside the door, trembling with anger.

Abruptly she reached out and picked up the ashtray that sat by the telephone and threw it across the room as hard as she could. It banged against the wall, gouging a depression in the plaster, then clattered to the wooden floor. That wasn't enough. She yanked up the lightweight wooden straight-chair and raised it above her head, then flung it down.

Three loud thumps sounded from the upstairs apartment. She stood by her door and stared at the ceiling. Her breath came in sharp little pants, but slowly, gradually her rigid muscles relaxed. She pulled off her coat and dropped it on the floor and wiped away the thin film of sweat that glistened on her face.

Martin was a fool, a fool, a fool!

And he had the gall to tell her that she didn't understand! Well, she understood plenty. She understood that Billy Kessler had loused everything up. She understood enough to know they had been betrayed. She understood enough to know that they had to do something or be laughed at. Why, everybody would think they were paper tigers if they let Larsen and Billy get away with it!

She crossed her small living room and yanked open the drapes and looked across the street at the two-story business buildings—and at the third building from the corner and the basement steps that led to Billy and Annette's apartment. She looked down and hated Billy.

Whirling around, she paced back across the room and her anger at Billy and Martin fed on itself. She had tried last night, right after everybody had walked away from the Greenway, to persuade Martin that they must do something quickly and he had shaken his head and said there was nothing they could do now, that they must wait.

There was plenty they could do, but he had been so sharp, so final that she had given way. But this morning the editorial in the *Gazette* changed everything! As soon as she had seen the editorial, she had hurried to Martin, to show him.

She stopped mid-way in her frenzied pacing and pulled the crumpled copy of the *Gazette* out of her pocket and opened it to the editorial page, and her eyes ran greedily down the column and fastened again on the words she had shown to Martin:

. . . disillusionment breeds violence. If the system shows itself incapable of simple justice, then who knows what will be the result. But if the frustration brings trouble, then Billy Kessler must shoulder much of the responsibility for . . .

It was plain as plain, Kathryn thought. The editor was saying there had to be trouble! But Martin didn't see it that way. Instead, he had smiled and said, "This is great. We'll let Stuart get everybody riled up, then when Billy's big debate with Larsen doesn't budge ROTC, we can call another rally. And we'll get a strike that time."

Kathryn had fought him and that was when he'd said she didn't understand.

She began to pace the floor again, her stride short and quick. Martin was the one who didn't understand. Rally, hell. They didn't need a rally. They needed something big. Something that would show they meant business. Her eyes swung toward the shiny black footlocker that sat by the window. Her steps slowed and her face furrowed with indecision. Was now the time? Or was Martin right? She didn't want to jeopardize Martin's hopes. She stopped in front of the footlocker and stared down at it, then jerkily turned away.

The editorial Saturday morning was, if possible, tougher than the one that ran Friday. Jake didn't quite go so far as to call Billy a turncoat but he came close to it.

In the narrow room at St. Catherine's, Annette didn't see either Friday's or Saturday's *Gazettes.* She sat in the hard chair by Billy's bed and watched the flush of fever mount on the sunken face and held a paper-dry hand and prayed. She slept some, but when he moved or moaned she would waken and rise and bend close.

Suzie saw both papers and she stayed away from the newsroom and she grieved for Jake's anger against his friend.

Kathryn hurried to the Union on Saturday morning to get a copy of the *Gazette.* She grabbed one up and opened it directly to the editorial page. She read and a sentence leaped up at her:

. . . know that violence is to be deplored. But if oppression is so great that the only recourse is violence, who can expect anything else? Because of Kessler's stand, the . . .

She read the editorial through twice, standing in the lobby of the Union. And then her eyes fastened again on those special words—*the only recourse is violence.*

She read the editorial once again when she was home in her apartment, then she lifted her eyes to stare at the footlocker near the window. And when she moved, she moved briskly, purposefully.

It didn't take long to assemble what she would need: the crowbar from the car trunk, a medium-sized claw hammer, a pair of pliers, the finely honed sharp knife with a six-inch blade.

She stacked the tools neatly on the floor, then lifted up the hasps and opened the footlocker. She set the yellow wooden box on the floor and next to it the metal spool with its weight of thick orange line. Again she put the circular tin across the room.

Jaime had explained the properties of dynamite to them one hot summer morning. He had held up a stick of dynamite, turning it around and about to show to them. Then he had flung it as hard as he could against the opposite wall.

The instant of terror had been acute. But the stick bounced off the wall and fell to the floor—and it didn't explode.

He had laughed. "*Mis amigos*, it takes the little explosion to set off dynamite," and Kathryn had learned that dynamite is detonated by the explosion of a small metal cylinder called a blasting cap. Dynamite can be dropped, thrown, and burned, but it shouldn't explode until rocked by the shock and heat of an exploding blasting cap.

The circular metal container held a hundred detonators, and they were highly volatile and to be handled carefully indeed. She wouldn't even remove their cover until the very last moment of preparation.

For now, it was time to open the wooden case. She picked up the crowbar and rested it against the seam of the box, then jammed it into the wood by a sharp blow with the hammer. Then she levered the bar up and down, and gradually the wooden lid began to give.

Kathryn took her time. All the compulsion for frantic haste had ended now that her mind was made up. She worked the crowbar around the lid, first on one side and then the other until the whole lid came free.

She stared down at the double row of dynamite and she felt the same instant of surprise she had experienced that summer day in Cuba. The cartridges were eight inches long and an inch-and-a-half in diameter, short stubby sticks about as thick as a man's thumb and so easy to hold. She had always pictured dynamite as looking like a huge red firecracker.

But no firecracker had such power. She held a cartridge in her hand and felt the slickness of the brown waxed paper in which it was rolled.

Her eyes narrowed as she concentrated and, once again, she could hear Jaime's light, mocking voice. "To make a primer and that, *mis amigos*, is an explosive with a detonator inserted, you first take the blasting cap and slip it over the end of the fuse. Then with pliers, you . . ."

Step by step, Kathryn remembered—and did.

19

ONE MORE MINUTE

In his modest, two-bedroom frame house on the east side of town, Sergeant Ronald MacIvor savored his beer and watched with mounting excitement the Saturday Night Movie. The jewel thief balanced on the narrow ledge, then with consummate grace climbed up the drainpipe and crawled in the open window and crouched behind the filing cabinet and waited for the slow footsteps—Sergeant MacIvor suddenly sat bolt upright. Filing cabinet. He thumped his beer can down on the Formica top of the endtable and swore.

His wife looked across the room. "What's wrong, Buddy?" He was already standing up. "I forgot to put this file away. I'd better go back and do it."

"On Saturday night!" she exclaimed. "Surely it can wait 'til Monday morning."

"No. See, the colonel got all hot to have better security. You know, since the riot on the Greenway. So he's started what he calls Emergency Procedures for the Duration." The sergeant grinned. "I think he's doing it all to bug Major Skelly. Anyway, all files pertaining to ROTC goals have to be kept locked up. But the major makes me lock them up because he'd feel put down if he had to do it."

MacIvor pulled on his leather jacket and checked to be sure he had the building key. He might think the colonel's new orders dumb but it never occurred to him not to go put the file away. He knew whose rear would be in a crack if the file were found by the colonel Monday morning.

"Hurry back, honey," his wife urged. "I'll make some doughnuts."

So Sergeant MacIvor straddled his Kawasaki and roared off toward the campus, fighting a gusty north wind all the way.

At the Mobil gas station four blocks west of the campus, Kathryn's beat-up Chevy coupe edged up to the regular tank. She unrolled her window all the way and, when the attendant came, held out a one-gallon gasoline tin.

"Some people up the road ran out of gas and I said I'd bring them some. Then will you fill my car up?"

"Sure, miss." He filled the tin first and brought it to her, then he put the nozzle in the gas tank. The tank was full long before he finished with the windows and checking the oil and battery water. She wanted to shout at him to hurry.

Finally, finally, he replaced the nozzle, then came around the car. "That'll be $4.85, miss, counting the gallon in the tin. Do you save stamps?"

"No," she said shortly. On the way to get her change, he stopped to pick up a chamois that had fallen from a water drum. A wild flash of irritation surged through Kathryn, but she fought it down, controlled it. This was not the night to be angry. Tonight she wouldn't let anything upset her. Not tonight.

So she managed a tight smile as he painstakingly counted out her change. By the time she had maneuvered the old car into the street, she was swinging back into a good humor because everything was working out beautifully. She flicked a satisfied glance at the picnic basket that rode on the seat beside her and at the gasoline tin riding on the floor.

She turned into the campus on Hurlburt and passed the Administration Building, all its windows dark, and the Graduate College, the Geology Building, and Pulitzer Hall, the tall graceful light-spangled Architecture Building, and Gilbertson Memorial Library, the only building lighted from top to bottom.

She passed the dark Greenway, only patchily illuminated by street lamps. In a street lamp at the far end, she could see the squat sandstone armory. She had really wanted to blow up the armory, but her reconnaissance that afternoon had shown it was impossible. The only access was by either the front or back doors. The occasional windows were high and inset in the thick old walls. But the ROTC office and classroom buildings to the west of the armory—they were another matter altogether.

She drove slowly, but she passed no one. When she turned from Hurlburt onto Dodson, the street lay empty and quiet. There, fifty yards ahead, lay the three wooden buildings used by the ROTC. She turned in on the blacktopped drive that led to a huge parking lot shared by the ROTC staff and the Home Economics faculty. She switched off her car lights and the old car nosed its way to the far end of the lot. She parked it next to the Frost Street exit. If she could reach the car quickly enough, she would be out on Frost and heading off the campus before the sirens could wail and the fire engines lumber down Hurlburt.

Sergeant MacIvor roared onto Dodson, but he didn't bother to rumble past the buildings to the parking lot. Instead, he braked his cycle right by the door of TB (Temporary Building) #2, the central building where Army ROTC officed.

He unlocked the front door and moved briskly down the central hallway, not bothering to turn on the overhead lights. He knew the building and he had excellent night vision.

His office was an interior one. It was an anteroom, really, to Major Skelly's office. He flicked on his office light and breathed a sigh of relief when he saw the file on the corner of his desk. He began to walk toward it.

Kathryn's sneakers made no sound as she walked swiftly across the blacktop toward the rear of TB #2. The black of her sweater and slacks melded into the night. Her right arm curved protectively around the picnic basket. Her gloved left hand gripped the gasoline tin.

She paused in the shadow of a fir tree directly behind TB #2. The wind rustled the fir and the other trees nearby. She could smell rotting leaves. But the long wooden building sat dark and quiet.

Kathryn walked softly up to the casement window to the left of the back door and very carefully eased the picnic basket to the ground beneath the window. Then she moved quickly to the end of the building and a little beyond it to the low mimosa tree that grew there.

She checked the street but it still lay empty. Then she stepped up into the tree's crotch, and holding the tin in her left hand, moved up a sturdy branch that stretched right up to the eaves of the roof.

She unscrewed the cap to the tin. Then, keeping her balance with her right hand against the bole of the tree, she waited for a lull in the wind. When it came, she swung the can so that the gasoline arched through the air to splash onto the old, wind-dried shingles.

When the tin was empty, she quietly worked her way back down the mimosa. Back at the window, she set the empty tin down beside the basket. Lifting the lid of the hamper, she pulled out a pair of wire clippers, a down pillow, and a ball peen hammer. She gripped the clippers firmly and began to cut away the bottom half of the window screen.

Toward the front of TB #2, Sergeant MacIvor stood in his office, clutching the manila folder and swearing.

The filing cabinet where the folder belonged was in Major Skelly's office. MacIvor had the key to the cabinet, but for some peculiar reason Skelly had locked his office door and MacIvor didn't have the key to that office. The stocky sergeant stood by the locked door, his face drawn in a half-worried, half-angry frown.

If he couldn't get in the major's office, he couldn't lock the file in its cabinet. But he had to lock up the file! If the colonel found out that the file had been out all weekend . . . Well, the colonel just wasn't going to find out.

Sergeant MacIvor swung on his heel and hurried to the old-fashioned wall safe that nestled in the corner behind his desk. He would put the file in there and first thing Monday morning he would sneak the folder into the proper cabinet. If anybody—like the colonel—ever found out it had been in the safe, he would claim that he thought the secret files were supposed to be kept in the safe and he hadn't . . .

He worked it out in his mind, foreseeing what might happen, what would probably happen, and what could possibly happen. Crouching in front of the old iron safe, he began to work the dial. Beads of sweat glistened on his face. His fingers slipped and he pushed the dial too far to the left. He swore, cleared the dial, and began again . . . 27 right, 31 left . . .

At the back of TB #2, the window glass shattered in the east storeroom, but the pillow muffled the crackling as the hammer struck and the tinkle as the glass shards fell to the floor wasn't loud enough to reach Sergeant MacIvor.

Kathryn held the pillow and the hammer and waited a long moment. Satisfied that no one had heard, she put her tools down to the left of the basket, then stood and reached a gloved hand through the now-empty frame and twisted the latch to unlock the window. This done, she eased up the bottom half of the window.

Not a sound, not a movement came from the pitch dark room beyond the opened window. Kathryn pulled a tiny pencil flash from her pocket and flicked it on. She rapidly searched the room, then turned the little light off. And smiled.

It was a storeroom, obviously. A tarp lay neatly folded in one corner. Nearby, two wooden ladders balanced against the wall. A row of paint cans was stacked against the far wall.

She nodded in satisfaction, then she knelt down by the hamper and with the utmost care lifted out an oddly-shaped package about eight inches long and five inches in circumference. It was a grocery sack wrapped tightly around five sticks of dynamite, then taped and taped again. The center stick was the primer. The 1½-inch blasting cap was firmly wedged in it. Crimped to the blasting cap was the safety fuse. The six feet of safety fuse was looped loosely around the outside of the sack.

She put the package down just to the right of the hamper. Then, quickly and efficiently, she laid the ball peen hammer, the wire cutters, and the pillow into the hamper. Reaching over it, she retrieved the empty gasoline tin and wedged it in one end, then closed the lid and put the basket just to the right of the open window.

Now she was ready. She picked up the oddly-shaped, taped package. She stood and leaned inside the window and used her flash to see a place to set the dynamite, gently, gently. Then she swung a leg over the window sill and climbed inside.

She picked up the package and crossed to the line of paint cans and set it down right in the center of the line of cans. Then, very carefully, she unrolled the safety fuse. From the instant she lit the fuse, she would have three minutes. She looked over her shoulder, making sure nothing barred her way to the window.

The matchhead flared, sharply bright, and she touched the flame to the exposed powder core of the fuse end. The powder ignited in a quick, brilliant flash and then it began to burn within the orange covering, the unseen flame eating its way toward the blasting cap.

Kathryn dropped the used match, jumped to her feet, and ran to the window. She clambered through it, grabbed up the picnic hamper, and pelted across the blacktop, a dark shadow in the darkness of a windy night.

In his office, sweat trickled down Sergeant MacIvor's face, but finally he heard the sweet, solid click as the combination worked. He pulled open the safe, picked the folder up from the floor and stuck it inside, then slammed shut the safe door.

He stood up with a sigh of relief. For a while there, he hadn't thought he was ever going to get that combination to work! But his usual good humor reasserted itself now that the crisis was past. He even whistled as he turned off the light and walked up the hall. He closed the front door behind him, double-checked to make sure it was locked, then hurried down the steps to his motorcycle. He revved it up and rode across the grass to bump over the curb. He was close to the corner when the tremendous whanging concussion slammed into his back, tossing him chest first over the handlebars to slam heavily onto the pavement.

Stunned, his right shoulder dislocated, his head gashed, he dimly understood that a massive explosion had occurred. He fought to retain consciousness. Pulling himself awkwardly up with his left arm, he looked back as a huge sheet of flame swept up and over the building he had just left.

The leaping flames crackled. The wind blew tongues of fire toward the nearby wooden buildings. Fire began to run in ripples across the roofs of the two other buildings.

TB #2 was an inferno of flame and noise and heat.

He looked at the wildness of the destruction and felt a sudden emptiness inside him. If he had been in his office one more minute . . .

"God Almighty," Sergeant MacIvor breathed softly.

20

THE ROOM SHOOK

The *Gazette* covered it like a horse blanket, six stories on page one and arty cuts of the charred remains of the three ROTC buildings and the fire-damaged roof of Home Ec. The chief engineer estimated the loss at $80,000.

Gazette editor Jake Stuart could scarcely conceal his satisfaction. He worked hard on his editorial for the Monday morning edition. Sunday evening he showed the copy to Suzie, who had come to the newsroom to help cover the blast.

She had taken it with a smile and then her face had drawn into a frown, and when she had read it she said flatly, "*Jake*, you can't print that!" The minute the words were out, she wished that she could pull them back. But the sharp, accusatory words were said and his chin was jutting out. "Sure I can," he said stubbornly, and he took the copy back.

And he did. Monday morning's editorial recapped the student demands for banning ROTC, then ended, "If legitimate protests are not heeded, the university invites rebellion. Perhaps

Saturday night's bombing of the ROTC buildings means that the kids are still trying to get the administration's attention."

The *Gazette* hit President Larsen's desk on Monday morning just shortly before he received the call from Governor Macklin.

The president listened intently, his face somber. "No, Governor, I can't promise you anything. I can't promise that someone won't blow up the Administration Building this afternoon. Or my house tonight. Or the Governor's Mansion tomorrow. I can't promise anything to anybody, but I have made what arrangements I can. I have ordered continual patrols of the campus, special attention to the nighttime security of all buildings, and I have appealed to the students for help in solving this crime. And I have pointed out very strongly that Sergeant MacIvor was spared only by grace Saturday night."

The telephone crackled again.

President Larsen said quickly, "No, Governor, I don't want troops. I think the arrival of troops would quite likely aggravate a bomber."

But when he put down the phone, he wondered how long he would be able to hold the governor off and keep his campus free from troops.

Down at St. Catherine's, Billy Kessler heard about the bombing and he urged students to help solve the crime. A reporter for the largest state daily managed to get to Billy's room. Billy was mending, his fever gone. He pulled himself up from his pillow and spoke quickly, emphatically, urging students to remember that violence was evil whether it happened in Indochina or at home. He would have talked longer but Annette quietly and determinedly backed the reporter out of the room.

* * *

Kathryn read every word she could find on the bombing and watched reports of the blast on TV. She hugged success to herself. She stayed away from her usual places and didn't answer her phone just in case Martin figured out that she was responsible and tried to stop her.

The interview with Billy wasn't published until Tuesday afternoon. She read about it over her dinner at a small café and she heard the students in the next booth hoping the police caught "that awful bomber" soon. The interview with Billy was picked up by the Wednesday morning *Gazette* and Rusty also ran the results of a campus poll that more than 90 percent of all students queried supported Kessler's stand against the bombing.

Kathryn read with a growing anger. Then a small boxed item at the bottom of the page caught her eye.

Billy Kessler, editor of the *Wilderness Voice*, who was injured in the Greenway confrontation last week, will be released from St. Catherine's Hospital Thursday afternoon.

Wednesday afternoon Kathryn paced up and down her living room, stopping occasionally to stare down at the basement grille across the street that marked Billy's apartment.

So the big deal with the big mouth would be home tomorrow. The fine liberal leader who wanted to see the bomber caught. The betrayer.

She thought it through, and she controlled the impulse to slip through the darkness of the night. Someone would notice lights in that apartment if she went there at night. She would bide her time . . .

Thursday morning she went to Dubois Hall, the chemistry building, and walked briskly to the supply storeroom on the third floor and waited until the graduate student on duty locked up to go for his coffee break. When the hall was empty, she moved close to the door, worked the lock for a moment with a helpful thin-bladed tool, and opened the closet. She found what she needed and was several blocks away when the graduate student returned.

The door to Billy and Annette's apartment opened at her first try. She stepped inside and her eyes darted all about the room, but it was empty. An afghan was crumpled in a heap at the end of the sofa. Piles of newspapers were stacked along one wall. The smell of mimeograph-machine ink mingled with the pungent odor of overripe bananas.

Sure now that the apartment was empty, Kathryn closed the door behind her. She set a shopping bag on the coffee table and pulled out the prepared clump of dynamite—five sticks again all taped together and the center one primed. She held that handful of death and destruction and turned around to study the front door. Her eyes searched near the door and fastened on an old-fashioned magazine stand that sat beside an easy chair. She crouched by the stand and with gloved hands lifted out enough copies of recent issues of *The New Republic* and *Evergreen Review* to make room for the dynamite. She loosened the length of fuse and hung it over the back of the stand, then covered the cartridges with a couple of magazines. The extras she pushed under the easy chair.

The safety fuse uncoiled easily like the quiet slide of a snake. She ran the bright orange fuse out of sight behind the magazine stand, then tucked the rest of it under the edge of the rug until the tip-end poked out near the door.

Kathryn knelt by that tip-end of the fuse and turned her head to the right to study the door, which opened inward. Yes, it was going to work.

She rose and crossed to the shopping bag and pulled out a small glass bottle. It was no more than two inches tall and a half inch in diameter. It was tightly stoppered. As she walked back to the door, the oily-looking yellow liquid rolled inside the little bottle.

Kathryn bent down and set the little bottle on the floor just past the fuse. Then she reached to her right and pulled the door in. As the door swung toward the wall, it came closer and closer to the little bottle. When the door was almost against the wall and the bottle hidden from view, it tipped against the small glass container and knocked it over. The lid held the oily yellow acid inside its glass prison. If the acid had spilled out onto the powder, the solid core would have ignited and begun to burn within its plastic cover.

Quickly she shoved the door shut. Then, carefully, deliberately, she took the little bottle, unscrewed its cap and set the bottle next to the fuse. She knelt yet a moment longer, re-checking the entire sequence in her mind.

She nodded in satisfaction. When the door opened , she got up briskly, dropped her tools in her grocery sack, rolled the sack into a neat compact length ,and stuck it in her pocket.

She moved quickly across the room without a glance at the colorful profusion of paperback books or at the bright balls of yarn tumbled on the small table beside the granny rocking chair. She didn't notice the basic cleanliness of the room beneath its thin coating of dust.

Not seeing, not caring, Kathryn reached the back of the room and opened the door to the narrow stairs. She shut the apartment door behind her, walked softly up the back steps, and slipped out the ground-floor door into the alley.

In the basement room, sunlight danced through the barred windows that opened onto the street. The sunlight shone on the asphalt-tile floor and on the white wooden table with its vase of dried flowers—and on the bright sharp colors of the magazines heaped so untidily atop the old-fashioned magazine stand.

Thursday afternoon, Jake Stuart sat in his office and felt as isolated as an astronaut on the moon. Maybe more so. Because everybody is at least for the guy on the moon. And Jake knew he couldn't count anybody in his corner. Man, was he ever persona non grata! And all because he wasn't hailing Billy as the hero of the decade. Well, he wasn't having any. Why couldn't everybody see it the way it was? Billy, Big Billy, the leader in the anti-ROTC movement, standing there and telling everybody it didn't matter about the blood on the Greenway. That wasn't justice. That was an old-fashioned sellout. God, he'd never been so wrong about anybody!

Jake shoved his chair back from his desk and pondered the loneliness of anybody who told the truth about things. With every editorial he'd written, he'd lost another friend. Jake stared out across the newsroom. Rusty had barely spoken to him since yesterday's editorial.

Jake looked past Rusty. His eyes were drawn to the sleek black head bent over the old Smith-Corona on the first row. Jake frowned and his broad face was wistful. Then, without giving himself time to think about his pride, he pushed up and out of his chair and opened the door and strode across the room.

He walked briskly, then pulled up short by Suzie's desk as if he had just noticed her.

"Hi, Suzie."

She looked up and when she saw he wasn't glowering as he had been for so many days, she smiled happily.

"Hi, Jake."

He looked down at her copy and rapidly read the first few sentences of her story, a feature on a visiting professor of music from Italy. "Almost finished?"

She nodded.

He looked nonchalantly at his watch. "It's almost five. How about a beer and a hamburger?"

"I'd like to," she said quickly, then she added reluctantly, "I have an errand I have to run."

"Something to pick up?" he asked good-naturedly. "Maybe we could . . ."

She shook her head and said quietly, "I'm sorry, Jake, but it's Billy. I have to go downtown and bring Billy and Annette home from the hospital. Annette doesn't drive so I . . ."

But he was already nodding and saying shortly, "Sure, sure. Well, some other time maybe." And he walked away. He stalked past Rusty's desk without saying a word, his head lowered, his face hard.

He yanked his jacket down from a peg near the door, then hurried up the hall to the stairs. But once outside the building, buffeted by a cold wind raw with the hint of snow, he stood uncertainly on the sidewalk. No place to go. Nothing to do. He walked moodily across the campus, not even zipping up his jacket, taking a kind of perverse pleasure in his own discomfort.

He sighed unhappily. Suzie had almost spent more time holding Billy's hand than had Annette. You'd think Billy was married to Suzie.

That thought didn't help any.

He reached the main gate of the campus and passed through it and crossed Boardman, then stood on the corner and tossed possibilities up in his mind. The book shop? A movie? Pizza?

He wasn't hungry. He'd just as soon be dead as go to a show by himself. And the paperback bookshop was crowded with couples.

He hunched his shoulders and turned into the wind and hurried two store lengths to Nick's Bar. He pushed into the dimness and sat on a worn red bar stool.

"Bud."

"One?"

He almost asked if he looked like he had two mouths but he only nodded shortly. "Yeah."

He drank one beer and glowered up at the wall-mounted color TV. The local news flashed on and his mouth twisted in disgust. Those guys wouldn't know news if they fell over it. News to them was something they read in the papers. He ordered another Bud and fought down the impulse to go back to the *Gazette* office. He knew when he wasn't wanted. So he drank his beer and watched the performing tube boobs and felt very put-upon indeed.

Suzie drove carefully, trying to avoid bumps, easing up to stop signs. She managed to keep on smiling, hiding from Billy and Annette the grayness that had enveloped her since Jake had walked angrily away. If she frowned or spoke shortly, they might think she regretted her promise to bring them home. And she wouldn't for the world hurt their feelings. So she smiled though she felt like crying and listened to Annette's happy chatter.

"And the doctor said Billy has to get a lot of rest but I've talked to all of his professors and got all the assignments and I can read everything out loud and everybody's been so nice . . ." She ran down for a moment, then reached over to touch Suzie shyly on the arm. "And you've been so great, Suzie, even though I know . . ." Then her words tumbled off to an awkward pause.

"Know what?" Suzie asked absently, wondering if it would do any good to call Jake after she delivered Annette and Billy.

"I mean, I'm sorry Jake is . . ." And her voice trailed away again.

Billy spoke up for the first time. "Jake doesn't mean all that. I know what's eating Jake. He's such a softy that he can't take it that people got hurt on the Greenway and nobody is having to pay for it. Jake'll be all right."

Suzie looked at him gratefully. In a way, she felt sure Billy was right, that Jake would see that Billy's way was best. And then she remembered again the ugly little editorial that all but said that bombing was great and she wondered tiredly if Jake would ever admit he was wrong. It would be very hard for him to do it. Her smile slipped away and she sighed.

Billy saw her frown and he knew what was wrong. He tried to think of something to say that would bring a smile back to her face. He couldn't make things right about Jake, but maybe he could at least brighten her day some other way. And he put away the thought of stretching out on his couch with the hi-fi turned just right and a steaming huge cup of Annette's spiced tea and a long, happy, lazy evening at home.

He didn't say anything as Suzie backed the Mustang into a slot a quarter of a block down from the apartment. He reached for his kit bag, but Annette already had it in hand and was holding the door for him.

"I can manage doors now," he said with a grin, but they walked slowly up the street. Annette hurried down the cement steps and unlocked the door, then turned and waited for Billy and Suzie.

Her thin face glowed with contentment as she exuberantly pushed in the door. "Suzie, come in and have a cup of tea with us. I'll start the water right now. It will only . . ."

Then Billy slipped his arm around her and his voice boomed out in the old loud sure way. "I have an even grander idea. Here Suzie's hauled us home and she's brought you sandwiches all week. What say we take her up the street for one of Mario's extra special pizzas? That sounds good, doesn't it? And we're sure to run into a lot of our friends and it will be a fine way to spend our evening."

Annette stood stiffly in his grasp for an instant. Then his big hand squeezed her shoulder and she understood that for some reason this was what he wanted, so she smiled too, though all she wanted was to be home with him.

Suzie protested that he should rest, that they could take her out another night, but Billy had the door shut and had turned them about and they were climbing up the front steps.

The acid, tossed down when the door first opened, had splashed onto the powder train. A little flame spurted up for an instant and then the fire began to eat its way inside the fuse.

Nick's Bar was down the block and around the corner from the basement apartment that Billy and Annette rented.

Jake was raising his hand to signal for his third Bud when the room shook and plaster fell in patches from the wall and the orderly rows of glasses on the counter behind the bar rattled and clinked and those near the edge tumbled over to crash on the floor.

The violence of the shock still sounded in Jake's ears as he flung himself off the bar stool and lunged toward the door.

Because he knew. Oh God, he knew what had happened before he ever hit the street.

"Suzie!" he shouted. "Suzie!" He ran to the corner and turned it and forced his legs faster and faster. He could see the tumbled heap of rubble mid-way up the street where a bakery had stood. The second story had belonged to a milliner and the basement to the *Wilderness Voice* and Billy and Annette Kessler.

"Suzie, Suzie!" And the call was deep and harsh in his throat because he saw the heap of clothing bundled on the sidewalk not far past the empty hole that had been a basement apartment. Jake ran harder than he had ever run before, then dropped on his knees to gather up that crumpled heap.

Bright clothes that afternoon in the newsroom. A red-and-white striped coat. A red scarf. Bright clothes only moments ago.

He held her limp body in his arms and smoothed the wiry coal black hair away from her face—and she stiffened in his grip and moaned and opened dazed and frightened brown eyes. She tried to struggle up and he understood the horror that she feared and he looked quickly around, then said, "They're OK, Suzie. I see them. I see Billy and Annette and they're OK."

She struggled for a moment more and then she understood his words and she sagged back in his arms and looked up at him.

He held her even closer and his eyes pled for forgiveness. "Suzie, I was wrong. I was so wrong."

She nodded, then reached up and gently touched his lips with a scratched hand. "Maybe somebody was trying to get your attention, Jake."

For a moment he was stricken by her words, then slowly he nodded. "Maybe somebody was."

Epilogue

"There is no magic about explosives. When fired, they simply change into another form, largely gaseous, having many times the greater volume. This increased volume exerts both a blow and a pressure on the confining material. It is this action which is effective in blasts. The pressure acts equally in all directions but the gas tends to escape along the path of least resistance, or the easiest way out. All explosives . . ."

It was this characteristic which saved Billy and Annette and Suzie. They had turned and left and shut the big, strong, old-fashioned door—and when the charges exploded, the tremendous force volleyed away from them. The easiest way out.

Not everyone was so lucky. Manuel Cordoba ran the Eclair Bakery. He was working on number 2 oven when the cartridges blew. The floor fell through and he was pinned beneath six hundred pounds of rubble. They got Mrs. Cordoba out alive and the milliner, Mrs. Griffin. Billy's shoulder had to be reset. Annette's neck was sprained and her left hip dislocated. Suzie's right arm was fractured and two fingers in her right hand were broken.

Kathryn had watched the building quiver, then collapse, but her eyes were fastened on the three who had started to walk away.

And she had seen them tossed forward to tumble down like rag dolls. But she had seen them get up again, too. It was then that she flung away from the window to throw herself down on the couch.

She heard the wail of sirens, fire engines, police cars. She heard shouts and commands and later, much later, she heard the tinkle of broken glass being swept up.

She lay on the couch and stared sightlessly at the ceiling and her thoughts were black and bitter. Once during the night someone knocked sharply on her door, but she stayed very still and finally footsteps walked away. The police? Because her apartment overlooked the street?

She had worried the rest of the night. And when the gray half-light of dawn filtered into the room, she pushed up from the couch and began to pace up and down across the room. What if the police searched all the apartments in the area? She stared at the dark shadow beneath the window which was the footlocker.

She walked to the window and looked out and watched the red circular light on the police car flash around and around and around.

They might have policemen knocking on every door. They might come back!

She hurried into her tiny kitchen and found a sturdy sack. She took it back to the footlocker, then lifted out the yellow wooden box. She dumped the dynamite sticks and the fuse spool in the sack and then she held the varnished yellow box and tried to think what to do with it. Thankfully, she remembered the incinerator on the roof.

She didn't even stop to pull on a coat but ran up the hall and to the third floor and then to the narrow steps that led to the roof. She only began to feel a little safe when the box was stuffed well inside the incinerator.

Back in her apartment, she put on her sneakers and draped a

coat over her shoulders and grabbed up the sack. She ran light-footed down the hall to the narrow back steps that led down to the fire exit. Once outside in the alleyway, she looked nervously around, then hurried past the garbage pails to the small parking lot. She fumbled with her keys and unlocked the trunk and shoved the sack inside, then slammed the trunk down.

"Hey, you."

Her shoulders stiffened. She turned slowly around and waited as the policeman walked up to her.

"You live around here, miss?"

She nodded.

"Where?"

She pointed back up the alley at the apartment-house exit. "There. On the second floor."

"What's your name?"

"Ellington. Kathryn Ellington."

He flipped open a small notebook, checked a list, then nodded. "OK, miss. This block's off limits for everybody but residents and shop owners until we finish sifting the wreckage."

She stared at him, her eyes wide and dark.

He said quickly, "Now, don't be scared, miss. These kind of killers don't come back. They set off bombs and run. You're not to worry."

She nodded, a pulse fluttering in her throat. And when he had walked away, she steeled herself not to run, but once upstairs in her apartment, she stood with her back to the door, her breathing ragged.

Sharply, the telephone rang.

She stared at it. Then, gulping in air, she ran across the room and snatched it up.

"Kathryn." Martin's voice was quick and hard.

"Yes."

"Kathryn. pick me up at the corner by my house." And the cradle clicked down.

She held the receiver in her hand and stared at it, puzzled. She had avoided him after she set the charges in the ROTC buildings. She hadn't answered the phone or gone to any of her regular places because she was afraid he might know she was the bomber and he might order her to stop. And now he called and asked her to pick him up.

She tried to re-create the sound of his voice in her mind. Firm. Tough.

Had he seen how the bombing impressed people? Was he toughening up? Could he be pleased?

She felt a surge of hope for the first time since she had watched in an agony of frustration as Billy and Annette and Suzie walked away from the apartment.

She whirled around and grabbed up her purse—and her eyes fastened on the bright red can of detonators. She hesitated, then hurried to the kitchen and snatched up another sack. She poured the detonators, ninety-eight shining copper shells, into the sack. She looked at the tin for a moment, then shoved it under the couch and it was hidden by the seat covers. She would get rid of the tin later. What mattered was not to leave the detonators in her apartment where they might be found.

When she was in the parking lot, she looked around carefully to make sure the policeman wasn't nearby, then she opened the trunk, hurriedly thrust the sack in, and slammed down the trunk lid.

The paper sack toppled over on its side and some of the detonators slipped out as Kathryn started the old Chevy and slammed into reverse.

Two shiny copper shells rolled close to the trough at the front of the trunk where the wiring for the brake lights nestled.

Kathryn drove fast. She squealed to a stop in front of Martin's house, and he was there and pulling open the door and sliding into the front seat.

"Let's go," he ordered.

She put the old car into gear and it lunged forward. The shiny copper shells tumbled into the trough.

Kathryn looked at him and the hope that had carried her to meet him withered and died.

"All right," he said harshly, "where's the dynamite?"

She slid him a wild look and drove a little faster. She could hear the thump of the heavy sack of cartridges as it tipped over. She laughed. "Dynamite?" she repeated. "What dynamite?"

He was coldly furious and utterly determined. He reached out and gripped her arm—and it hurt.

"Listen, do you think I don't know?" And he swore at her and called her a fool and said he would take the dynamite away from her.

The old car racketed up the street. She drove fast and faster and then she was on a blacktop that led out of town.

In the trunk, the dynamite slithered and slid as she drove wildly, recklessly. It was an old car, worn out in many ways. Kathryn drove it to prove that she didn't want money, didn't need money. The tires were worn almost bald in spots. The brake drum had been turned. The wiring on the brake lights was worn, the insulation cracked in spots. One of the shiny blasting caps had wedged against worn wiring.

Martin's pressure on her arm increased. Angry now, goaded too far, she slammed on the brakes. The red-hot wire touched the powder that had broken out of the jounced shell.

For a split instant, there was a tiny dance of flame, a minor flash of heat, then the sack of blasting caps exploded, touching off the huge, whamming, final explosion.

About the Author

Carolyn Hart, an accomplished master of mystery, is the author of twenty previous Death on Demand novels. Her books have won multiple Agatha, Anthony, and Macavity Awards. She is also the creator of the Henrie O series which features a retired reporter, and the Bailey Ruth series which stars an impetuous, redheaded ghost. One of the founders of Sisters in Crime, Hart lives in Oklahoma City.

CAROLYN HART CLASSICS

FROM OPEN ROAD MEDIA

OPEN ROAD
INTEGRATED MEDIA

www.ingramcontent.com/pod-product-compliance
Lightning Source LLC
LaVergne TN
LVHW090608110826
845146LV00001B/306

* 9 7 9 8 3 3 7 2 0 3 9 6 6 *